JEKKA WILDE

ACE OF SPADES

THE WICKED BOYS OF WONDERLAND

BOOK ONE

Cover design by Wilde & Free

CONTENTS

CHAPTER ONE

ALICE

Vibrant strobe lights flashed across the sea of writhing bodies on the dance floor, casting a kaleidoscope of colors onto the polished surfaces that surrounded me. The bass-heavy music thumped in my chest, each beat threatening to steal away my breath as it filled up the room.

My nostrils were struck by the scents of sweat, perfume, and alcohol, creating a heady concoction that only served to calm me down. I only felt at ease when I was drinking and partying, and Château Noir was the hottest club in LA. By some miraculous stroke of luck, I'd managed to get in without anyone realizing who I was.

The anonymity was lovely.

Sheer heaven.

And I wasn't about to give it up.

"Hey Alice, are you ready for me to call us an Uber?" Dinah shouted through the thumping house music from the barstool beside me.

"Fuck no!" I yelled back to my personal assistant. "I'm not nearly drunk enough yet!" I waved a hundred-dollar bill at the bartender, less worried that he'd recognize me and more concerned that he wouldn't replace my vodka gimlets as fast as I was pounding them down.

The humiliation was still too new, too painfully raw. My social media accounts were blowing up so bad that I'd turned off my phone a couple hours ago.

They say it's not about the cards you're dealt, but how you play them. Well, I'd been dealt a winning hand—maybe the best hand you can possibly get—and somehow I'd managed to completely blow it.

I wasn't an idiot.

I was just unlucky.

Really, really unlucky.

I say I was dealt the best hand of cards because my entire family is famous. Like, *insanely* famous. My dad is Derek Darling, a retired big-shot NFL quarterback. My mom is Valentina Darling, a world-famous supermodel. My parents raised me and my sisters in Malibu . . . on 'Darling Dynasty,' a reality TV show that's been running forever. It's been filming since my parents announced they were expecting their first baby.

I hated growing up in front of the cameras. Kids at school would only be friends with me because they thought I'd help make them popular or because their parents thought my parents would make them popular. Most people only saw dollar signs when they looked at me. I guess word got out that if me or my sisters were invited to someone's birthday party, your odds of getting an insanely awesome gift were all but guaranteed.

Things only got worse with puberty, and everything that went along with it, like boys, acne, and tits that seemed to appear out of nowhere. Boys never liked me for who I was. They just liked the idea of who they expected me to be.

Also, the tits.

Mine were impressive.

And I had them before most other girls had theirs. Which resulted in tons of teasing, and being accused of having a boob job in junior high, etc.

As fast as my tits grew, my friends from grade school transformed into mean girls. Then the mean girls turned into sadistic bullies that made my life hell. And all of my angry outbursts and awkwardness was captured on film for the entire world to see on endless reruns of *Darling Dynasty*.

Fast forward to our twenties, and my older sister Marcella had a leaked sex tape that launched her into a booming swimwear and lingerie company. My younger sister Bianca took some cues from our mother to start her own modeling career *and* created a makeup brand that was dominating all the others.

And I . . .

Well . . .

I was still the unluckiest member of our family.

I wasn't driven to hustle like Marcella was. I wasn't handed every opportunity on a silver platter like baby Bianca. The only things I was really good at were shopping, drinking, and fucking.

So when Remy, my venture capitalist boyfriend, gave me the opportunity to invest in a business and help me launch my very own line of shoes, I jumped at the chance to create my own empire.

Instead of being famous for falling out of limos and puking on red carpets, I could have a legitimate business of my own, just like the rest of the Darling Dynasty.

All I had to do was help design pretty high heels, strappy sandals, and then show them off on my social media sites. As long as I bankrolled the project out of my trust fund, Remy promised to take care of the details and make me a success.

Sounded like a win-win.

It turned out to be a raging dumpster fire.

After only a week since my company's official launch, everything blew up like a fucking supernova for the entire world to see.

I didn't think it was possible for one man to fuck me in so many ways—and I *loved* fucking, so this genuinely caught me off guard—but Remy made it look easy.

I woke up that morning to a text from Bianca.

How are you doing?

Just woke up.

Have you checked your socials yet?

No. Why? Are people excited for the launch? I hope we have enough inventory. Although if we sell out of the 'Daddy's Girl' heel I think it would increase demand/visibility. OMG—what if the website crashes???

. . .

Just check your IG

FUCK

WTF??? THAT FUCKING SHITHEAD ASS FUCKER POS DOUCHE CANOE!!!!!

FML

I'm so sorry, Alice. I'm still in Milan but LMK if you wanna talk.

K

Apparently, when my boyfriend said he'd take care of the details, what he really meant was that he was too busy fucking his side chick to bother doing any actual research on *how* the shoes were made, *where* they were made, or *who* was making them.

No, Remy thought his time and my money were better spent by flying to Ibiza with his mistress and making sex videos, which got leaked onto a handful of porn sites. He'd spent so much of *my* money trying to get the videos taken down that he could only hire the cheapest suppliers to make my shoes—the shittiest sweatshops in the world.

You know, the kind that made complete garbage and paid underage kids pennies a day to mangle their little hands.

And all of this was blowing up during the week of my big launch.

I did my best to do damage control, but the news about Remy . . . well that was the shit cherry on top of the shitty icing of this whole shitty sundae.

My personal assistant Dinah had come to my rescue with one of her magic smoothies.

"Give me your phone and I'll take care of it," she said, trading me for a big neon blue glass of delicious oblivion. Dinah always denied it, but I swear she put Xanax in her smoothies because they made me forget all about my troubles for hours and hours at a time.

The feeling started to wear off while I was in the limo on the way to my family's annual charity gala.

"Can you hand me my phone?" I asked Dinah. "I need to look over the notes for my speech."

"Sure," she said, handing it over.

I didn't look at my notes. I went straight to all my social media pages and read the endless streams of nasty comments.

People online were either tagging me in video clips of my boyfriend's side chick getting plastered in the face with cum, or sharing videos about the shitty quality of my shoes. Buckles were breaking, soles were flapping around as they came unglued, and rhinestones were popping off right out of the box.

I know I said this was happening during the week of my brand's official launch . . .

But did I mention this was happening while I was hosting my family's annual charity gala . . . for *exploited children*?

You know, the same kind of kids like the ones who were making my shoes?

Yep.

I'd been dealt an incredible hand at life and completely blew it.

I was booed off the stage in less than a minute, and every miserable second was photographed and plastered on the internet before I scrambled behind the curtain.

I booked it for the nearest bathroom, where I watched my relationship, my reputation, and my fledgling shoe company implode in a Twitter shit-storm from the safety of a toilet stall. I didn't know how to fix the problem, other than calling Remy, only to find out he'd ghosted me.

By the time Dinah found me and convinced me to crawl out of the bathroom, I was convinced that getting shitfaced as fast as possible was the only logical solution.

Why did I ever think I could be the queen of my own little kingdom?

I didn't have what it took to be a queen.

I was a fucking joke.

"Here, take this," Dinah said, pressing one of her familiar neon blue pills into my hand. "It'll make you forget all about this shit show. You'll feel like your old self again in no time."

I didn't hesitate. I'd taken plenty of Dinah's

'happy pills' since she'd started working for me. They had the same effect as her smoothies did. I tossed it into my mouth and washed it down with the fresh gimlet sitting in front of me.

What did I have to lose?

The promise of escaping my humiliation was all I could think about as I watched the writhing bodies on the dance floor. The bass pounded in time with my pulse, and that neon blue pill slid down my throat, leaving a trail of numbness in its wake.

I shivered involuntarily as a wave of warmth seeped through my body, chasing away the chill of humiliation that had clung to me all evening. For a brief moment, I thought it might be working—this magic blue pill of forgetfulness that Dinah had given me.

But then the memories returned with the force of a thousand thunderstorms, and I knew I was still trapped within my own private hell.

At least nobody at the club had recognized me yet. That was the last thing I needed.

"Are you drunk enough for us to leave now?" Dinah shouted at me.

I shook my head.

"Nope. I'm gonna need a couple more before I'm ready to go home," I told her. She rolled her eyes at me, but I had no fucks left to give.

"Whatever. I'm going to the bathroom. You good?"

"I'm fine!"

She shot me a look that said she didn't believe me, but I didn't care.

"Be right back," she said, sliding off her stool and disappearing into the cacophonous crowd. I stared blankly at my empty gimlet, my thoughts swirling like the melting ice cubes in my glass.

The second she disappeared in the crowd of sweaty club kids, a man with bleached white hair tried to take her seat.

"Sorry, dude," I told him while shoving my Birkin bag where Dinah's ass had just been. "My friend's sitting there."

The man's pale gaze studied me as if he'd recognized who I was. I narrowed my eyes and turned back to my fresh drink, sipping it slower this time. At least he wasn't paparazzi.

"Alice?"

"Nope."

"Come now, Alice . . . I'd recognize you anywhere," he said in a posh accent that grabbed my attention. He took out a shiny gold pocket watch and looked at the time. Then he set it on the bar and frowned at me in disapproval. "You're terribly late."

I glanced down at my long, side-swept cascade of perfectly highlighted blonde waves that led to the plunging neckline of my ruffly blue cocktail dress. With a name like Alice, I knew exactly the reference he was making.

It was pretty ironic, given that he was dressed in all white and had bright white hair. His impeccable suit looked completely out of place amidst the glitter and sweat that filled the nightclub.

"Yeah, punctuality isn't exactly my best feature," I slurred, accidentally spilling vodka into my lap. "Let me guess—you must be the White Rabbit. Are we late for a very important date?"

"Oh, that date has come and gone," he scoffed, although there was a concerned edge to his voice. His eyes flicked impatiently between me and the gold pocket watch he held in his trembling hand. "Alice, you aren't just late. You are *years* behind schedule!"

"*Years*? Wow . . . " I said, marveling at his commitment to the joke. "Either you're one hell of a method actor, or you're on some *really* good drugs."

"Terribly sorry, Alice, but I'm no actor. I'm here to escort you to Wonderland." He leaned in closer, his voice low and urgent. "You're very, *very* behind schedule. Time is of the essence."

"Look, Mr. Rabbit—" I squinted at him, trying to discern any ulterior motives but finding none— "I'm glad you're having a good time tonight, but I'm not about to leave here with a stranger and go to a second location. My life might as well be over right now, but I don't feel like getting murdered."

He blinked curiously at me.

"Murdering you? Why, that's the very last thing I want to do to you."

I rolled my eyes.

"Whatever. I'm not interested in fucking you."

"Nor am I interested in fucking *you*," he replied

with a sudden fierceness that made me pause. I suddenly realized he didn't play for my team.

"Please don't misunderstand me," he clarified, a hint of distaste creeping into his voice as he glanced at his pocket watch once more. "I have no interest in seducing you, Alice. My concern lies solely in saving Wonderland. I'm frustrated by how dreadfully late you are."

I narrowed my eyes at him, feeling oddly relieved by his apparent disinterest in my body. I'd met plenty of weirdos in Los Angeles, but none quite as unique as Mr. Rabbit. He looked so posh and out of place in his pristine white suit, surrounded by the grime and debauchery of this nightclub in downtown Los Angeles.

Plus, the way he looked at me was a welcome change from the usual leering stares I attracted. He looked at me like I was someone important.

Not famous or notorious. *Important*, like he respected me.

Like I was a queen.

I started to let down my guard.

"Fine. I'll play along," I sighed. Despite my inebriation, I couldn't help but be intrigued by the man's commitment to his role. He seemed harmless enough. And what did I have to lose? I'd already lost everything else. "Tell me more about saving Wonderland."

"Time is running out for all of us who live there," he explained, his voice tinged with urgency. "And *you*, Alice, are the key to saving it."

I folded my arms across my chest, purposefully pushing up my tits. Mr. Rabbit's eyes never wavered from mine. Impressed with his genuine lack of sexual interest, I raised an eyebrow at him.

"You said I was late. Tell me more about that."

"Time is a fickle thing in Wonderland," Mr. Rabbit explained, his fingers drumming anxiously on the bar top. "For us, years may have passed, but for you . . . it's like no time has gone by at all. However, your absence has left a void that is tearing our world apart. You must understand, Alice—you are our last hope."

"Me?" I scoffed, swaying slightly on my barstool. "You've got to be joking."

"I'm deadly serious," Mr. Rabbit insisted. "Your role in Wonderland is not just important—it's absolutely crucial!"

"Is it now?" I smirked, the alcohol in my veins making me bold. I leaned in closer to Mr. Rabbit, my breath nothing but fumes of vodka. "And what, pray tell, does this 'crucial role' entail?"

"Ah, well, that's the thing," Mr. Rabbit stammered. His gaze flickered to the dance floor, where sweaty bodies writhed together in an erotic display. "It's rather . . . complicated."

"Of course it is," I drawled, rolling my eyes. "It's always complicated."

I chomped on an ice cube while Mr. Rabbit launched into a sales pitch that made hardly any sense to me. He talked about some bitch called the Red Queen, who basically went insane and started beheading everyone who lived in her kingdom. Her sister, the White Queen—how creative—did her best to control her, but apparently she was too far gone to fix.

Then Mr. Rabbit mentioned something about a battle between demons and fae, some weird mutant pet of the Red Queen's called a Jabberwocky, and a magic sword.

My eyes glazed over as he spoke, and the longer he went on, the more fascinating his story became.

"Is this guy bothering you?" Dinah asked, putting a hand on her hip as she took in Mr. Rabbit's pristine white suit and expensive-looking watch.

"Not at all," I slurred, waving a careless hand in his direction. "He's got some crazy story about me being late for some epic battle against the Red Queen in an alternate universe called Wonderland."

"Really?" Dinah replied, her voice carefully neutral. But there was something off about the way she was suddenly fidgeting with her purse, avoiding eye contact with Rabbit. I squinted at her, suspicion creeping through my drunken haze.

The second Mr. Rabbit caught Dinah's gaze, he tensed up and pushed away from the bar, nearly knocking over the stool as he sprinted towards the door. Dinah let out a sigh of relief.

"Hey, do you know him or something?"

"Me?" Dinah laughed, perhaps a little too loudly. "No, of course not. I've never seen him before in my life."

"Good," I said, nodding once. "Because if you were keeping secrets from me—"

"Never," Dinah interjected, her voice fierce but her eyes still evasive. "Forget about that freak. It's getting late. How long do you want to stay out?"

Just then, I noticed the golden pocket watch was still sitting on the bar top. I grabbed it before anyone else had a chance to steal it and take it to a pawn shop.

"Hey, Rabbit!" I yelled through the crowd, waving his pocket watch in the air. "You forgot this!"

All I saw was a flicker of white darting through the door to the club.

My pulse quickened, the thrill of the chase igniting something primal within me, and I charged after him with renewed resolve.

Dinah grabbed the pocket watch and tried pulling it out of my hands.

"What are you doing?" I asked, not letting go. "I need to give this back to him! It looks expensive. Maybe it's a family heirloom."

"Then he shouldn't have left it laying around," Dinah argued, trying to wrestle the watch from my grip.

"What the fuck's wrong with you?" I snapped, anger flaring beneath my inebriated state. "I'm giving it back, and you're not going to stop me!"

With that, I wrenched my body away from Dinah's greedy hands and stumbled out of the night-club and onto the rain-slicked streets of Los Angeles.

I was, determined to return the pocket watch to its rightful owner.

I didn't realize how drunk I was until I was out on the sidewalk. Rain pelted down mercilessly on me as I stood outside the club, my once pristine blue cocktail dress now sticking to me like a second skin. The cold droplets mingled with my anger and frustration, fueling my determination to return the pocket watch to Rabbit. I couldn't explain why it felt so important, but something deep within me told me that it was vital he get this thing back.

I clutched the watch tightly, its cold metal biting into my palm. I scanned the streets for any sign of Rabbit, feeling a mixture of anxiety and excitement bubble up within me. And then I saw it—a flash of white, barely perceptible amidst the neon-lit chaos.

With newfound purpose, I stumbled forward, following the fleeting figure through a labyrinth of dark alleyways and unfamiliar streets. My heels clicked against the wet pavement, echoing through the night like a metronome counting down the moments of my life.

"This is insane," I muttered to myself, feeling the absurdity of my actions. "Chasing a guy I don't even know, all because of a damned pocket watch."

The twisted shadows seemed to dance around me as the city's darkness closed in, threatening to swallow me whole. But I pushed onward, driven by a burning curiosity that refused to be extinguished. I could feel the weight of the watch growing heavier with each step, as if it were a ticking time bomb just waiting to explode.

And then I saw it: an old mansion looming before me, hidden away behind a veil of overgrown foliage and crumbling walls. It was a relic of a bygone era, standing defiantly amidst the modern skyscrapers that had long since encroached upon its forgotten domain.

"Seriously?" I sighed, my voice dripping with both disbelief and exhaustion. "How have I lived here my whole life and never noticed this place before?"

My gaze followed the figure in white as he slipped through a side door, leaving it open just enough for me to see the warm light spilling out onto the rain-soaked ground. The temptation was undeniable; I could either stay out in the rain, or follow Rabbit into the unknown warmth of the mysterious mansion.

"What the hell?" I whispered to myself, taking one last glance at my soaked dress. "I've already come this far."

With a mixture of trepidation and resolve, I approached the door, my hand reaching out to push it open. As I stepped over the threshold and into the unknown, I couldn't help but wonder if I had made a terrible mistake. Visions of ax murderers danced in my head, but somehow that didn't squash my curiosity.

The door creaked open, its hinges groaning like the wails of a thousand lost souls. The darkness beyond seemed to pulsate with a sinister energy that threatened to consume me, yet I found myself unable to resist the siren call of the unknown.

"Fuck it," I muttered, my breath fogging in the chilly air. I took a tentative step forward, crossing the threshold into the abyss. But as soon as my foot touched the ground, the floor seemed to vanish beneath me, and I was plunged into an endless freefall.

My screams of terror echoed down the dark abyss as I plummeted into an inky void. My golden hair whipped around me like a shattered halo, and my blue cocktail dress was shredded to ribbons with every jagged edge that I encountered. I clawed desperately at the cold, slimy walls, feeling the fabric of my designer heels rip from my feet before they were swallowed by the darkness.

Just when I thought the fall would never end, I slammed into the soft, damp earth with a sickening crunch, gasping for air as my body protested the impact. Groaning, I rolled over onto my back and stared up at the dismal sky gray overhead.

The twisted landscape stretched out before me like a battlefield, dark and surreal. The flowing grass was replaced by gaping chasms of decayed roots where mushrooms, mold, and oozing black sludge bubbled up from the depths below. Ancient trees with gnarled branches reached out like bony fingers, their bark torn and crusted in moss. The flowers clung to the ground with wilted husks, their petals blackened and decayed.

My gaze swept across the horizon, taking in the acidic lakes that bubbled and hissed with noxious fumes, their surfaces marred by the carcasses of unfortunate creatures who'd dared to drink from their depths. Black mountains loomed ominously in the distance, their peaks oozing a sickly yellow substance that seemed to poison the very air.

"What . . . what was in that blue pill Dinah gave me?" I whispered, my voice trembling with equal parts fear and excitement. My words were immediately carried away by the fetid breeze as I took my first tentative steps into the heart of darkness.

As I ventured further into the strange realm, the plants and trees grew thicker, forcing me to sidestep between shattered mirrors and creeping vines. Thorns grazed my skin, leaving angry red welts in their wake. Panic bubbled up inside me, threatening to burst forth, but I swallowed it down, reminding myself that I'd chosen this path—for better or worse.

This wasn't Los Angeles, and it wasn't any place I'd visited in my childhood dreams. It was a nightmarish hellscape that threatened to devour me whole.

And yet, despite the terror gnawing at the edges of my mind, I couldn't shake the feeling that I'd been here before.

As I picked myself up from the ground, it occurred to me that maybe this dark, twisted place was the perfect reflection of the darkness within my own soul. The emptiness I'd felt for so long.

Yeah, I had cars and clothes and a killer bachelorette pad, but when it came to friends and boyfriends, I was a broke-ass bitch. Because of my famous family and our connections and money, sooner or later everyone who came into my life proved that they didn't actually give two shits about me. Just like my venture capitalist fuck buddy, people only wanted whatever I could get for them. Influence. Connections.

Power.

The void in my life seemed to be mirrored in the decay that now surrounded me, and it both terrified and exhilarated me.

As I went deeper into the macabre landscape, shadows of twisted shapes danced around me, teasing and taunting. The scent of rot filled my nostrils, making me gag. Yet, there was something oddly intoxicating about it all.

I stepped cautiously over the gnarled roots that somehow seemed to have become conscious of my presence and were groping for me in the darkness. Skeletal trees loomed above, their bare limbs swaying ominously in the breeze.

Somewhere in the distance I heard a strange, low moan—like something from another world. The air was thick with a pungent stench of decay that burned the back of my throat as I took a deep breath. I could feel my heart racing in my chest, a mixture of fear and excitement coursing through my veins.

A familiar voice cut through the oppressive darkness. I followed it until I pushed through some decaying shrubs and found Mr. Rabbit standing with two other men, locked in a heated argument.

My sudden presence seemed to startle them, as if they thought they were alone. Mr. Rabbit was so surprised to see me that he actually jumped.

"Un—fucking—believable," muttered one of the men under his breath as he stared at me. He was smoking hot.

Literally.

There was a big swirl of soft blue and green smoke wafting around him that smelled like blueberries and mint. There was also a hard, lean sharpness about his features . . . something about him that both scared me and intrigued me. His deep teal hair was shaved on the sides and swept back in a slick pompadour.

Colorful tattoos crawled out from beneath his rolled-up sleeves, licking along his neck like snakes, leaving an unsettling feeling in my gut. He lifted a cigarette to his lips, glaring at me with undisguised loathing.

Mr. Rabbit, on the other hand, eyed me doubtfully. "I can't believe you're actually here," he hissed, his hands trembling. "You're so very, very late."

I opened my mouth to retort, but then I noticed the third man studying me with a mix of desire and curiosity. His tousled black hair crept down to his shoulders, and he wore a tuxedo covered in black and silver leopard spots that made his every movement shimmer with magic.

But it was his eyes that were impossible to look away from. They were a brilliant shade of bright green and they seemed to penetrate my very soul, making me shiver involuntarily.

"Why hello, Alice," he purred, the sly grin on his face both seductive and menacing. "Welcome to Wonderland."

CHAPTER TWO

ALICE

“So, the Ace of Spades finally decided to show up,” the teal-haired man sneered in a sardonic tone. "How very . . . untimely of you, Alice.” His eyes were cold and calculating as they bored into mine. In that moment I realized there was nothing ordinary about this man.

“What the actual fuck is going on here? Is this some kind of twisted cosplay?” I demanded, trying to ignore the way my heart skipped a beat at the gorgeous, slightly feral men eyeing me like prey. "What is this place? And how the hell do you know my name?"

“So many questions, and so little time,” Mr. Rabbit said, stepping closer to take his pocket watch from me. “Perhaps introductions are in order first. My name is Winston, and these are my associates. Chess,” he gestured toward the man with the sexy smile, "and Callister.”

The colorfully tattooed man took a long drag off

his cigarette and fixed his sullen eyes on me with disdain.

"Everyone in Wonderland knows who you are, Alice," he drawled as sweet-smelling smoke curled around him. "Not that it matters now. You don't stand a chance in this godforsaken place."

I bristled at his cold dismissal, but my anger was quickly replaced by intrigue as Chess came forward. A seductive grin played across his devilishly handsome face, and his green eyes sparkled like emeralds, beguiling and dangerous.

Though he appeared human, there was something feline about his movements, something predatory. An ache of longing tore through me as his gaze lingered on my body, and I forgot all about Remy.

"I believe you'll do just fine navigating Wonderland . . . with a little help, of course," he purred, his voice sending shivers down my spine. "This realm is unlike anything you've encountered before. But fear not. I shall be your guide through its dark depths."

"Oh, we all know *exactly* what dark depths you're going to help Alice navigate," Callister shot at him.

Chess laughed softly, ignoring the jab. He was so close that I could feel the warmth radiating off of his body.

Somewhere in my dark depths, I began to stir.

"Don't mind Callister. He's a shifter, so he's extra grouchy since he's about to go through his metamorphosis."

I frowned in confusion.

"What do you mean by metamorphosis?"

"He's like a phoenix," Chess replied with a nod. "You know, that mystical bird of fire who is reborn again and again from the ashes . . . except the bird is a butterfly and the ashes are a caterpillar . . . and there's no fire . . . and he never dies. So," he paused, giving me a wide grin, "he's not like a phoenix at all, apart from having wings. Callister always gets tetchy around this point of his metamorphosis, right before he sheds his skin."

"Why don't you tell her all the rest of my dark secrets, you worthless Cheshire Cat demon?" Callister growled through his teeth. Chess either didn't notice or didn't care.

"Wait . . . you're a demon?" I asked him in disbelief. Chess turned to me, still grinning wide, and yet still so seductive.

Then, in a breath of air, he faded into nothingness. Right before my eyes, he completely evaporated.

Then he reappeared, leaving me speechless.

For about five seconds.

I was still pretty drunk, but this shit had me convinced I was starring in my own lucid dream. I decided to lean in and play along since it seemed like I'd be here for a while. I crossed my scratched-up arms over my chest.

"*These* are your associates?" I asked Winston, my brows furrowing in blatant skepticism. "A bitchy caterpillar and a demon cat fuckboy ?"

"Oooh, I've never been called *that* before, but I

like it," Chess replied, his hypnotic green eyes barely leaving mine.

"Leave her be, Chess," Winston warned, tapping his foot impatiently as he glanced at his pocket watch. His nose was making a nervous twitch. "There's no time for your demonic games of cat and mouse. We need to make Alice understand the importance of her presence here. There's no time to waste. No time at all."

"Fine, fine," Chess admitted as he backed away from me with a hint of reluctance. "But let it be known that my offer still stands. I will happily be your guide if you'll have me. If you *want* me."

Another ache twinged deep inside my body. I'd been planning on revenge sex with all of Remy's friends, but why bother when I could fuck a demon instead?

Could demons even fuck?

With every seductive syllable that Chess uttered, I was really starting to think it was possible. If this was going to be *that* kind of lucid dream, I wasn't going to say no to someone who looked like him.

"I'm glad that you're finally here, Alice," Winston said, slipping the gold watch into the pocket of his white pants. "We've been expecting you for years, but the cards were stacked against us. The fates have been conspiring for ages to bring you here, to our twisted Wonderland."

"You honestly think this is fate?" I asked, fighting the urge to laugh at the absurdity of it all. "This is insane. I don't belong here."

"Ah, but that's where you're wrong, my sweet," Chess whispered, his voice like velvet. "We've always had an Alice as our champion . . . our Ace of Spades in this grand game . . . but never one so . . . so . . . ."

"So fucking old," Callister snapped as he lit a fresh cigarette.

"The fuck?" I sputtered. "I'm only twenty-six!"

"Now, now, there's no need for rudeness," Chess said, wagging a disapproving finger at Callister. Then he turned back to me. "Alices aren't very common these days. It's such a shame Winston didn't find you sooner, back when you were still an innocent."

I thought about telling Chess that I hadn't considered myself innocent in over a decade, but Callister's voice cut through the air.

"She's not worth our time," he insisted. "Just look at her."

"What's *that* supposed to mean?" I demanded.

Callister let out a low, contemptuous laugh. Then he blew a blueberry-scented smoke ring that grew bigger and bigger as it floated over to me and turned into a mirror. I gazed at my reflection and sucked in a sharp breath. It was like a TikTok filter designed to make me look absolutely heinous.

My hair was a tangled mess, full dead leaves, rotting burrs, and slimy globs of sickly green mold. My blue cocktail dress had been torn to shreds, only clinging to my skin from the mud and sweat and slime caked on my skin. My arms and legs looked bony and frail instead of tanned and toned.

But my eyes were what startled me the most.

They'd sunken into my skull, leaving dark circles that no amount of concealer would've been able to hide.

"Is that what I look like?" I stretched out my arms and stared at my reflection, not knowing if it was actually me I was looking at.

"Yes. You're a fucking disaster," Callister said. He tapped the ashes off his cigarette and the magical blueberry smoke mirror scattered to the ground.

"We should give her a chance to play out her hand, now that she's here," argued Chess. "We don't know what she's capable of."

Callister shook his head so emphatically that some of his teal pompadour fell into his eyes.

"She's too old. How much imagination do you think she has left? I can't work with this."

"She might be about ten years too late, but she's here now. You know it's not just about imagination. It's also about luck. This Alice might surprise us."

"Or she could end up setting us back even more than we already are." Callister pushed his hair back into place and narrowed his eyes at me. "I just don't see her succeeding. She doesn't have the skills or the wit to take down the Red Queen."

"Hey!" I howled in drunken indignation. "I can be witty!"

Callister shot me a look that said he was unimpressed.

"I'd rather invest my time and effort in someone more reliable."

A low growl rose from the back of Chess's throat.

"The longer we wait for a better hand, the

further Wonderland falls into ruin. Is that what you want?" With a melodramatic motion of his hand, he showcased the rotting landscape around us.

Callister shifted uncomfortably from one foot to another.

"No, but—"

"Then why not see if Alice can be the champion we need? Let's give her a chance to be our Ace of Spades and help us win. Who knows? We might get lucky."

I grinned at those words, but I kept my mouth shut. I wanted to see how this all played out. Besides . . . I liked the way it felt to have Chess defending me.

Callister's frown wavered as he realized he was on the losing side of their argument, but he was still unconvinced.

"We can't rely on luck and chance. She needs to actually prove herself capable of the task ahead."

Chess raised an eyebrow as a cunning smile played on his lips.

"That's all I'm asking you for, is an opportunity to let Alice prove herself. You never know what someone is capable of if you don't give them a chance."

With a reluctant sigh, Callister blew a swirl of purple smoke into the air. It curled and morphed into the shape of a grape-scented dragon. Then he pursed his lips, his eyes flicking back and forth between me, Rayburn, and Chess.

"Fine. We can try, but don't blame me if it all goes wrong."

"Taking risks is part of life," Chess assured his friend. His green eyes were back to sparkling with mischief. "What's the worst that could happen?"

One of Callister's eyebrows quirked up and he tilted his head to one side.

"The Red Queen could cut off our heads. She could send her Jabberwocky to eat whoever was left. She could turn Wonderland into an even more putrid wasteland than it already is. She has the power to turn the lakes into acid and the rivers into blood. It's only a matter of time before she makes the mountains erupt with warm green glops of gangrenous pus."

The moment I heard those words, I swallowed back the urge to throw up. It felt like something was crawling around in my stomach and needed to get out. But I couldn't puke now. Not in front of these hotties.

"Could someone please explain exactly what you want me to help with?" I finally asked.

"Allow me to enlighten you on the current state of Wonderland," Chess began as he gracefully settled himself on a moss-covered tree stump.

"Once upon a time, Wonderland was a realm of balance and harmony, held together by the Red Queen and the White Queen–two sisters who each rule their own kingdoms. The Red Queen rules the Kingdom of Hearts and Roses, while the White Queen rules the Kingdom of Diamonds and Ice. They and their kingdoms are opposites in every way.

The Red Queen is vicious, cruel, and feared by all, while the White Queen is beloved and kind, although her generosity is often taken advantage of by others."

"Kindness is just another word for weakness," Callister added while sending a plume of grape-scented smoke into the air. The sweet smell was a sharp contrast against the decay all around us.

I was torn between agreeing with Callister and wanting to prove him wrong. Every time I tried trusting someone, I always ended up getting fucked over. Remy was a perfect example. People only seemed to let me down, and yet . . . I still kept hoping that someday my luck would change.

"It depends on the context of the kindness," conceded Chess before turning his gorgeous face back to me. "Unfortunately, Alice, you've been gone for so long that the balance of power between our two queens has shifted too far in the Red Queen's favor. The White Queen has been forced into hiding to save her life."

"We've always had an Alice to act as the fulcrum that keeps their power in balance," Winston explained. "But because it's taken me so many years to track you down, the Red Queen has manipulated things to her advantage. As you can see, her twisted darkness now dominates all of Wonderland. It might even be past the point of no return. That's why your arrival is of the utmost importance."

"I'm still not understanding exactly how I'm

supposed to help you fix this place," I said, motioning at the gnarled trees that clawed at the sky around us.

Callister let out such a wicked laugh that it made my skin buzz with electricity. I wanted to make him laugh like that.

"All you have to do is find the missing Vorpal Sword and use it to kill the Jabberwocky, which is the embodiment of all the Red Queen's power."

I kept waiting for Winston to laugh, but he was serious.

"No one else can slay the Jabberwocky," Chess explained. "It has to be you."

"If you were still a child, your vivid imagination would've allowed you to believe that you actually had a fucking chance," Callister said with a scowl. "But you're so old now that you'll shit yourself the second you lay eyes on the damned thing."

I tossed my tangled mess of slimy hair behind my shoulder and jutted out my chin in defiance.

"You don't know that," I said, putting one hand on my hip. "How scary is this Jabberwocky thing, anyway?"

"Terrifying," said Callister.

"Horrific," said Winston.

"The stuff of nightmares," said Chess, although he still didn't seem that scared. I assumed it was because he was a demon. Maybe the Jabberwocky was a cousin. "That's why we'll have to see how imaginative you are, and help you hone your skills."

"Hold on a fucking minute," I said, swallowing back another wave of nausea. "I've never slayed anything except my wardrobe, and now you want me to save an entire realm?"

"To put it simply . . . yes," Chess replied with an innocent shrug. "You are the key to restoring balance in our realm."

"Or destroying it," Caterpillar added darkly.

"Couldn't you find another chick named Alice?" I suggested. "A little kid with a better imagination?"

Winston shook his head.

"You were chosen to be our champion, our Ace of Spades from the moment you were born. It has to be you."

"Why do you keep calling me the Ace of Spades?"

"Simple," Chess murmured. "You are the luckiest and most powerful card in the deck. You've been missing for a very long time."

It almost broke my heart to tell them the truth, but I felt like I had to do it.

"Look, I'm not powerful," I confessed. "My family is, but I'm not. I'm a laughing stock. A complete joke. And I'm definitely not lucky. Not at all."

"Things are different in Wonderland," said Winston. "Your luck may very well be about to change. That's why I was able to find you after all this time. I'm still willing to bet on you, Alice."

"As am I," said Chess.

"I'm still deciding," growled Callister.

I stifled a burp and rolled my eyes. Something hellacious was going on with my stomach. Unlike the men who surrounded me, this sensation didn't make me feel good at all.

"If this would've been so much easier when I was still a kid, then why the hell did it take you so long to find me?"

Winston gave me an apologetic look.

"I've been searching for you for years, but someone's been dimming your light . . . essentially hiding you away from our view." Winston's eyes narrowed in frustration. "I think I know who's to blame."

"You do?" asked Chess. Winston nodded while casting suspicious glances at his companions.

"When I found Alice tonight, she was with Dinah."

"Dinah? Well, that explains everything," said Chess with a little snarl.

"I'm not following," I piped up. A fierce expression darkened Chess's green eyes.

"Dinah works for the Red Queen. She's most likely been keeping you distracted from visiting Wonderland."

"Wait, what?" I blinked in confusion. "Dinah is my friend! She's my personal assistant! Why would she . . . "

Before I could finish my sentence, another round of nausea hit me like a sledgehammer. Doubling over, I heaved a few times onto the ground, then found myself staring at the bright blue pill that Dinah had given me to forget my humiliation.

To my horror, it grew bigger and bigger, quivering

on the ground until it transformed into a shimmering fat worm and started to crawl away.

"Curiouser and curiouser," Callister mused under his breath. "I do believe it's heading for the Red Queen's castle."

"What the hell is that thing?" I gasped, my voice shaky. I felt as if the ground had completely shifted beneath my feet.

"A blue pill," he sneered before stomping it to death under his shoe. He wiped the goo on a moss-covered log before looking back at me. "It seems your 'friend' has a hidden agenda."

"A blue pill makes you forget everything that matters," Chess told me with a forlorn expression. "If Dinah told you to swallow that, she's not your friend. Has she given them to you before?"

"Yeah. Lots of times," I admitted. There was a sick, sinking feeling in my heart as I began to realize Dinah might be like all my other 'friends'—as fake as a fifty-dollar Rolex.

"Does she regularly give you anything else to eat or drink?" Winston asked. Callister and Chess both leaned closer to hear my reply.

I nodded, fighting back the tears of betrayal that were starting to sting the corners of my eyes.

"She makes me superfood smoothies every morning," I told the boys. "My freezer's full of them. Do you think she's been putting stuff in my food?"

"Without a doubt."

"It's not even a question."

"No wonder I couldn't find you for all these

years," Winston confessed with a weary sigh. "There is a light within you, Alice. A strength that connects you to Wonderland. But those blue pills from Dinah have blocked your connection to us here, which made it impossible for me to find you sooner. If you stay here long enough, you'll start to feel that strength, that connection once again."

And even though my mascara was running and I'd just puked all over the ground, my stomach started to feel better. I started to feel stronger. Even the air didn't smell that bad anymore.

"Well, if the Red Queen hasn't heard about your arrival yet, she will soon enough," Callister said, glaring at the blue smear on his shoe.

Winston shuddered.

"I really do have to run and inform the White Queen while there's still time."

He looked over at me, and I saw the seriousness of his expression.

"Will you help us, Alice? Without you, the Red Queen's power can't be checked, and Wonderland will fall deeper into darkness. She wouldn't hesitate to kill the White Queen."

"It's true," Callister admitted as he lit yet another cigarette. This time, soft swirls of pink cherry-scented smoke spiraled around him. "Wonderland needs you more than ever."

"What if I say no?" I asked. "Could I go home? Is that even an option, or am I stuck here?"

"There's a way home," Chess said softly. "You're

not a prisoner here, Alice. You are more important to us than any treasure."

"You're so fucking important that if you don't help us, you're essentially condemning us to this endless suffering forever," Callister growled, malice glittering in his eyes. "And forever is a very, *very* long time."

By this point I was pretty sure Callister was a sadist. There was no need for him to twist the knife in me like that, but he'd just gone and done it anyway. The pressure I felt weighed on me like a ton of bricks.

For being in the middle of a lucid dream, this one felt surprisingly real. Even my heart was thumping in my chest so hard that I could feel it.

"I'm not sure I can handle this level of responsibility," I stammered, wringing my hands together nervously. "You really expect me to find a magic sword, kill some monster called Jabberwocky, defeat the Red Queen, and save this . . . this hellish Wonderland? Just like that? It sounds impossible!"

"We don't expect you to get this all done in a single day," said Chess.

"It would be lot more impressive if you *did*," Callister jabbed, his voice dripping with disdain.

"That's enough out of you!" Winston snapped, his jaw twitching with irritation. "She's only just arrived, and already she's shown more courage than any of us were expecting! I thought surely by now she'd run away screaming."

"Oh, I thought about it," I confessed, shaking my

head in disbelief. "But it's not like there's a door anywhere around here."

"There's a way out of here, although Callister's not wrong," Chess explained to me. His warmth and captivating presence drew in my attention. "Without your help, the Red Queen will kill her sister and destroy what's left of Wonderland. But if you stay . . . " Chess's green eyes were gleaming with hope.

"If you stay, the impossible can become possible. I know you have the power to restore balance to our realm. We can't do it for you, but we can help you unlock that power. I will walk beside you every step of the way, should you choose to stay."

I nodded as I processed everything that they'd told me. I glanced from Chess's reassuring smile to the twisted, rotting world around me, knowing I stood at a crossroads.

One path would lead me back to Los Angeles, where I was a failure at starting my own business, a failure at relationships, and a failure at knowing who to trust.

The other path led into the darkness . . . into the unknown.

But at least here I might be able to make a difference.

The grotesque landscape of Wonderland stretched out before me like a sickly, nightmarish painting. Rotting flowers drooped around my feet, their petals oozing a viscous black ichor that seemed to burn the very air with its foul stench.

The trees twisted and gnarled overhead, blocking out any semblance of sunshine, casting an eerie half-light over the black mountains in the distance. Acidic lakes bubbled ominously nearby, warning me to watch my step.

As I stared into the trio's pleading eyes, I felt a spark of something inside me—a flicker of courage that refused to be extinguished. It was small, fragile, and barely perceptible, but it was there, waiting to be nurtured.

I bit my lip, my eyes darting between my strange new companions: Winston, desperate and urgent; Callister, cold and disbelieving; and Chess, warm and encouraging.

I took in the horror and decay that surrounded us, the overwhelming odds stacked against me, and finally made my choice.

"Fuck it," I said, my voice holding a newfound determination. "I'll do it. I'll stay and help save Wonderland. What have I got to lose?"

Callister let out a sinister laugh that intrigued me just as much as it concerned me.

"That depends on who you meet while you're here," he said with a wicked grin. "You might lose your mind or your heart . . . but I'd be most worried about losing your head."

CHAPTER THREE

ALICE

"Apologies, Alice," Winston said, glancing yet again at his pocket watch. "I must inform the White Queen of your arrival. Chess and Callister will take care of you."

"Wait!" I called out, my breath still heavy from the lingering effects of the gimlets I'd been drinking earlier. "What about the Vorpal Sword? You promised to help me find it."

"Callister and Chess will help you," Winston's words tumbled out as he backed away. "Tick-tock, Alice," the White Rabbit taunted, his voice somehow both playful and menacing. "Time waits for no one, you know."

He shot his friends a look that suggested they'd better follow through, then gave me a polite nod and disappeared into the dense woods.

"Okay . . ." I muttered under my breath, still unsure if this was all just a twisted dream or some bizarre reality. My head was swimming with equal parts excitement and fear. Was this dream, this strange Wonderland, really relying on me to save it?

I steadied myself against a nearby tree trunk, feeling the rough bark against my fingertips. As the booze began to wear off, my senses felt heightened, more alive than they'd ever been in Los Angeles.

One of those heightened senses was my nose, and I could smell the slime and sheer grossness coving my body.

"Can I, um, take a shower?" I asked, feeling suddenly self-conscious after my tumble into Wonderland. "I need to clean up before we go anywhere."

"Of course," Chess purred, his voice as smooth as velvet. He gestured to a knotted tree nearby. "Just step into the hollow of the tree, and it'll take you directly to our house."

I raised an eyebrow.

"You want me to walk into a tree?"

"Trust me." Chess's emerald eyes sparkled with mischief. "We may be miles from our home, but magic works wonders in these woods."

"Oh, I'm not surprised that you walk through trees to get to your house," I told him, glancing between him and Callister. "I'm surprised that you two actually live together."

"Well, Callister is an incredible cook," grinned Chess. "And he's very tidy. And he's been my friend as long as I can remember. I didn't exactly give him much of a choice in the matter."

"Unfortunately," Callister grumbled, taking a drag from his cigarette. "C'mon, let's get moving."

With my curiosity getting the better of me, I followed him into the hollow of the gnarled tree. My stomach lurched as I stepped through space, and a kaleidoscope of colors and shapes whirled around me.

Suddenly, I was standing in front of a breathtakingly bizarre house. It looked like an architect's fever dream–a mix of Gothic and Victorian with hints of Art Nouveau thrown in for shits and giggles. The windows were made of stained glass, depicting scenes of debauchery and delight, while the walls seemed to undulate and pulse as if they were alive.

My jaw fell as I took a few steps into Callister and Chess's front yard. I was immediately surrounded by vibrant colors and scents that I'd never experienced before. The lawn was a lush, vibrant green, speckled with wildflowers in all shades of the rainbow, and the trees were full of strange-looking fruits that glimmered in the sunlight. I could hear birds chirping happily from their nearby nests, adding to the symphony of life that surrounded me.

"Welcome to our humble abode," Chess announced, grinning mischievously as he led me to the front door and invited me inside.

The interior was just as breathtaking as the exterior. Every surface gleamed with an otherworldly glow. The furniture appeared to be made from living vines and branches, curling and twisting around one another like lovers entwined in an eternal embrace.

"The bathroom is this way," Chess said, guiding me down a hallway adorned with bizarre paintings of people and creatures I couldn't identify. He opened the door to reveal a surreal bathroom, complete with a purple bar of soap sitting on a stack of fluffy pink towels. There was even a new toothbrush waiting for me.

"Take your time," Chess whispered in my ear, his breath warm against my skin. "I'll have Callister make something to eat when you're ready."

"Thanks," I murmured, unable to take my eyes off the spectacular space. The walls were covered in shimmering tiles that seemed to shift colors with every blink, while the sink and claw foot bathtub resembled delicate seashells carved from marble.

As Chess closed the door behind him, I couldn't help but shudder at the thought of what might happen next. Wonderland was completely foreign territory to me, but I couldn't deny the pull it already had on me.

I stepped into the shower, sighing in pleasure and relief as the hot water cascaded over my body. Steam filled the room, enveloping me in a soothing embrace. I began to wash away the filth and grime that clung to my skin and my hair, watching as the muddy water swirled down the drain.

Grabbing a handful of silky shampoo, I massaged it into my scalp, allowing the suds to trickle down my neck and shoulders. I lathered up a soft sponge with the purple soap, inhaling the scent of lavender and something darker, more mysterious, and more intoxicating.

I stood under the torrential downpour of water, lost in the sensation of being made anew. It was as if I were shedding my past self, my old life with all its superficialities and regrets, and emerging as a stronger, more determined version of myself. The water rinsed away not only the dirt, but also my fear and uncertainty, leaving behind a fiery resolve.

I stepped out of the shower feeling reborn, the lingering remnants of my previous drunken haze now replaced with newfound clarity. Somehow, the fluffy pink towels weren't just soft . . . they were warm and cozy when I wrapped them around my naked body.

When I reached for my ruined dress, I found it had been magically repaired. The once-tattered blue fabric was now whole and pristine. A matching jacket had been set nearby, probably to help protect my arms from getting scratched up by the thorny vines. There was even a pair of gorgeous boots, their supple leather promising both comfort and protection.

But it was the transformation of my underwear that surprised me the most.

They were clean, and they were still hot pink and lined with lace, but now they had white letters embroidered on the front that said, 'Eat Me.'

Smirking to myself, I slipped them on. Maybe if I played my cards right, I'd get lucky and someone actually *would* eat me.

I quickly dried off and got dressed, admiring my

reflection in the mirror. This reflection was totally different than the bony, sickly woman I'd seen in Callister's smoke mirror.

Now I looked every inch the badass heroine, ready to take on whatever Wonderland could throw at me.

"Bring it on, bitches," I said, grinning at my reflection.

To my shock, my reflection put her hand on her hip, jutted out her chin, puffed out her chest, and replied, "You know they will. But I got you, babe. I got you."

I don't know what the hell was in that purple soap, but I dried off the bar and slipped it into the pocket of my jacket. I'd need some of this whenever I got back home.

Feeling more confident and determined than ever, I made my way to the kitchen, where Callister and Chess were sitting at a table piled high with delicious food. The aroma of cinnamon rolls, fresh waffles, sizzling bacon, and sweet fruit filled the air, making my mouth water.

"Ah, there she is," Chess hummed in approval, his green eyes taking in my physical transformation. "I trust you found everything to your liking?"

"Ohhh yeah," I replied, taking a seat beside him. "What the hell's in that purple soap?"

"Whatever you imagined was in it," Chess replied with a mysterious shrug as he poured me a cup of tea. "You look lovely, by the way," he continued, his gaze lingering on the curve of my thigh as it peeked out from under the hem of my skirt. "I took the liberty of repairing your dress, along with providing the new jacket and those rather fetching boots."

"Thank you," I said, feeling an ache in my core. I gave him a flirtatious grin and reached for a plate. "They're perfect. I appreciate the wardrobe upgrade."

"You're most welcome. I tried to find the perfect balance between practicality and showing off your gorgeous legs."

I laughed lightly at Chess's flirtatious remark, feeling a warmth in my chest that had nothing to do with the steaming cup of tea I'd just sipped.

Callister, sitting at the head of the table, scowled at the exchange. His jealousy was palpable, and I couldn't help but feel a sense of satisfaction in knowing I'd managed to get under his skin. I ignored the way his jaw clenched while Chess offered me a waffle and strawberries and syrup and juice. I could practically feel the jealousy radiating off him like heat from a fire.

But I couldn't bring myself to care. There was something about Chess–his magnetic charm, his wicked smile–that drew me to him like a moth to a flame.

While they chatted about various landmarks and which places to steer clear of, I shoved forkfuls of food into my mouth. I hadn't realized how hungry I was until I started eating, and now I couldn't seem to get enough. I'd destroyed half a cinnamon roll before I finally sat back in my chair. I closed my eyes, wishing with all my might that Callister would leave, or that Chess would take me to his room for a Cheshire Cat demon 'nap.'

"Are you going to sit around and daydream the time away," Callister sniped, his voice tight and strained, "or are you going to go and find that damn sword?"

"Easy, Callister," Chess chided, still looking fine as hell. "No need to be so tense. We're all on the same side here."

My eyes flickered sideways, catching Callister's dark expression. He sat slumped in his chair; one hand curled around a half-smoked cigarette that smelled like cartelized bananas. His other hand was picking idly at a piece of toast. His jaw was set, his tattooed biceps taut beneath the rolled-up sleeves of his shirt.

"Is there something wrong, Callister?" I asked, unable to keep the edge from my voice. "You seem . . . extra grumpy."

He glanced up, his hypnotic, yet cruel eyes narrowing as they met mine. "No, nothing's wrong," he replied, his tone clipped and harsh. "I'm just not convinced you're taking your duties seriously, that's all."

"Excuse me?" I bristled, setting down my fork with a loud clatter. "What's that supposed to mean?"

"It means that this isn't some game, Alice. We need someone who can actually make a difference," he retorted, taking a long drag of his cigarette before exhaling a plume of sweet-smelling smoke. "Not some spoiled, oversexed socialite who's only here to have a good time."

"Callister," Chess warned, his green eyes narrowing dangerously. "That's enough. Alice will get the job done."

"Maybe," Callister sneered, crushing the cigarette in an ashtray, the ashes scattering like his unspoken thoughts. "Or maybe she's just another spoiled brat who thinks she can waltz in here and save the day."

My jaw tightened at Callister's words. I'd never been one to back down from a challenge, especially when someone underestimated me.

"You guys asked *me* for help, remember?" I shot back, refusing to be cowed by Callister's hostility. "So, you can either get on board with the plan or shut the fuck up. Maybe if you weren't so busy smoking yourself to death, you'd be of some use around here."

"Ooh, feisty!" Chess exclaimed, his sly grin growing wider. "I like that in a woman."

"Fine, princess. I'll help you find that damn sword. But don't expect me to hold your hand every step of the way."

"Oh, I definitely don't," I said, wrinkling my nose in disgust. "As if I'd *ever* want you to touch me."

Callister's eyes locked on mine with an unspoken challenge I didn't quite understand. *Was* he jealous? Did he see something in the chemistry between Chess and me that he wanted for himself?

Or was it just that he couldn't stand the thought

of someone like me–a frivolous, uppity rich girl—having any power over him?

It was probably a little of both. My mom was a frickin' model, after all. I knew how hot I was.

I took a deep breath and turned back to Chess, leaning forward just enough to give him a great view of my cleavage.

"So, Chess . . . if I'm supposed to save Wonderland, where do I start?"

"First," he replied, his fingers tracing a slow, seductive path up my thigh, "you'll need to learn more about the Vorpal Sword. Where it's hidden, and then how to wield it, and what dangers lie between you and the perils of Wonderland."

"I can handle that," I agreed, trying to ignore the heat that pooled in my core as his touch lingered. Whatever was going on between me and Callister, I knew one thing for sure: Chess had me ensnared, and I had no intention of trying to break free.

"Chess," I began, biting my lower lip as my pulse raced, "will you come with me? Will you come along and help me find the sword? Show me what to do once I get my hands on it?"

His green eyes darkened, and a look of hunger spread across his face. "I'd be delighted, Alice," he purred, his hand still on my thigh. The contact sent shivers down my back, and I couldn't hide my sudden intake of breath. "You don't need to be shy about asking me for anything you want, Alice."

"Oh, I won't be shy." I looked away from him and

settled my gaze back on Callister, whose nostrils were flaring with restrained frustration.

Yeah . . . he totally wanted to fuck me.

"How soon would you like to leave?" Chess murmured, leaning closer until his lips were almost touching my ear.

"As soon as possible," I whispered, embracing the throbbing sensation between my legs, even though I was still looking at Callister.

"Then let's not waste any more time."

"Do we need to bring any supplies?" I asked, finally turning to look at Chess. His pupils were dilated with desire, suggesting that he might've liked to stay and show me his room. Instead, he took his hand away from my thigh and regained his composure.

"Anything we could need, I can provide," he boasted, and made a little motion of his hand. Suddenly he was holding an umbrella. He tossed it to Callister, who caught it and set it aside just in time to catch a purple flamingo, followed by a dozen baby flamingos. Then a pair of ruby slippers. A bouquet of cat-shaped helium balloons. A book of fairy tales and a bag of marshmallows. A pinwheel. An inflatable raft.

But when Chess hurled a bowling ball at him, Callister had clearly had enough.

"Will you stop it? You've made your fucking point!" he growled as he dropped the bowling ball on the floor with a heavy thud. The family of purple flamingoes flapped around him, each of them flying in different directions. One of them was digging through his teal pompadour.

I burst out laughing as Chess took my hand and led me down the hallway and out the door.

"I can't believe that just happened!" I gasped, trying to catch my breath. Chess shook his head and brushed a piece of lint from his leopard print tux.

"He brings it all upon himself. Honestly . . . he's so easy to tease. That's why I have to be creative in finding ways to make it more interesting."

"I've gotta say, I'm impressed by your creativity," I told him as we started to walk down the path that meandered across the front lawn.

"Just you wait, Alice," he said, placing his hand on the small of my back. "I'll show you just how creative I can be."

"Wait!" a voice shouted behind us, jolting me out of the sensual fog I was quickly getting lost in.

I turned around to see Callister walking towards us. He was waving something in his hand, but I didn't notice what it was because I was too distracted by the family of flamingoes following behind him.

"Here," he said gruffly, pushing the object into my hand. His expression was impossible to read. "This should help you on your journey."

It was a rolled-up piece of parchment.

I unrolled it carefully, revealing a very detailed map of Wonderland. A purple 'X' marked a spot deep within the twisting, labyrinthine forest, and I couldn't help but feel a thrill of excitement at the thought of what lay ahead.

"Aww, thank you, Callister," I replied, genuinely touched by his gesture. "This is really sweet of you."

"Whatever," he muttered, lighting another cigarette. The smoke smelled like grilled pineapples.

As much as he infuriated me, there was something undeniably magnetic about him—something that made me want to try my damnedest to figure him out.

One thing at a time.

One guy at a time.

For now . . .

"Is this where you think the sword is hidden?" I asked, tracing my finger over the 'X'.

"Perhaps," Callister replied noncommittally, blowing out a plume of golden smoke. "But be warned, Alice–that mark may not stay in one place for long. The map is . . . unstable. Unpredictable, much like everything else in this realm."

"Sounds about right," I said, folding up the map and slipping it into my other jacket pocket. As if anything in Wonderland could be straightforward.

"We should get going before it gets dark," said Chess. We walked to the edge of the yard, finding an unpaved road that forked in three different directions.

"One more thing," Callister called to us. I turned around and saw his cigarette was trapped in his lips while his strong arms were busy cradling one of the baby flamingoes.

"Yeah?" I asked, finding it impossible not to smile at him.

To my surprise, Callister actually smiled back.

Fine, fine.

So it wasn't exactly a smile. But the corner of his mouth was definitely twitching in that direction.

"Watch out for the fuzzy pink bunnies."

CHAPTER FOUR

ALICE

"What did Callister mean about the fuzzy pink bunnies?" I asked as Chess and I stepped into the fork in the road.

"He meant exactly what he said. Watch out for them."

Chess furrowed his black brow as he studied each of the three roads sprawled out before us.

"There are some ground rules you must adhere to if we're going to travel together."

"Really?" I asked with a flirtatious grin. "You don't strike me as the kind of guy who likes having rules."

Chess turned to me, and the hunger in his eyes made my knees tremble.

"I don't have many," he said, caressing my cheek with a few fingers. Then he cleared his throat and became serious. "Firstly, do not eat or drink anything you come across in Wonderland."

"Dude, I just ate brunch at your house," I reminded him.

"That was different."

"Why?"

"Because it was brunch at my house," he said, not going into further detail. "Secondly, do as Callister said and beware of the fuzzy pink bunnies."

"Seriously?" I scoffed, resting a hand on my hip. "What's so dangerous about fuzzy pink bunnies?"

"Trust me, Alice," Chess said darkly, the perpetual grin fading from his face. "They may appear small and harmless, but they are far from it."

"Fine," I said, rolling my eyes.

I redirected my attention to the road that spread in three different directions, then pulled out the map.

"Where are we?" I asked. "Can you point out your house on here?"

I followed Chess's fingertip to where three roads all came together. Then I looked at the purple 'X'.

"Looks like we should take that road," I said, pointing to the one in the middle.

"Then off we go."

Every step we took revealed something new and bizarre. I saw giant flowers that hummed sweet songs despite being eaten alive by black slime, towering mushrooms that thrummed with life, and trees that whispered secrets in the wind. It was all so intoxicating and surreal, like walking through a Salvador Dalí painting come to life. And even though I knew I should be cautious, I couldn't help but feel . . . alive.

"Are there cars here? What about horses? Walking seems like it'll take forever."

"No cars," he replied. "And horses tend to get noticed. The last thing we want is for the Red Queen to find out you're here."

"What'll happen if she does?"

Chess frowned.

I didn't like it.

"She'll send her headhunters after you. She might cut off your head, or she might turn you into a lamp post. It's impossible to know, so I'd suggest we walk and not get caught by the Red Queen or any of her minions."

"Some pointers on what to do in case of an emergency would be useful," I said, only half joking.

"To be honest, it all depends on you," he said, never breaking his stride. "You'll have to tap into the raw energy of your deepest, darkest fantasies. That's what powers everything in Wonderland. It' how the Red Queen became so powerful. You could be just as powerful, and then use that power for good."

"Okaaaaaay," I said slowly. "And how exactly do I access that power?"

"Let your mind wander, Alice. Let yourself daydream and explore the depths of your imagination. Don't be afraid to indulge in your most private, most twisted fantasies."

I felt a familiar ache as he mentioned any twisted fantasies I might have. I didn't want it to stay stuck in my head as a daydream. I wanted to ride him like a fucking hobby horse.

"Imagine using the fear of your enemies to strengthen your own power," Chess went on. "Or picture yourself commanding legions of ferocious creatures to bend to your will."

A smile crept onto my face at the thought, and I could feel something stirring within me. My curiosity was piqued, and I found myself more eager than ever to dive deeper into this strange new world.

"Does that seriously work?"

"It does, but I think you'll need to practice on smaller things before you're commanding armies," he chuckled.

"How small?"

"Imagine your dress is red, not blue," he suggested, slowing down his pace. "Can you do it?"

I looked down at my cocktail dress, which was the most intense shade of cobalt blue.

"I don't know. It's pretty bright."

"Just try," he urged, coming to a stop. "My clothes aren't covered in leopard spots."

"Yeah they—whoa!" I gasped, watching slack-jawed as his tuxedo changed from black and silver leopard print to purple and black tiger stripes.

"How did you do that?"

"I imagined it. Now try it with your dress."

Running my hand along the bodice, I closed my eyes and imagined a shade of red that I thought would look best against my skin tone. When I opened them, the top of the bodice was that exact shade of red, although it faded into purple and then blue by the time it reached my waist.

"Holy shit! It worked! Kind of . . . "

"Not bad for your first try," said Chess as he eyed my cleavage against the red fabric. "You look good in red. You'd look good in anything."

"How about a burlap sack?" I joked, picturing it in my head. The next thing I knew, my nipples were being scratched by rough brown burlap. I screamed in delight.

Suddenly I was pushed up against a tree, a warm hand pressed against my mouth. Chess was staring at me with such fierce intensity in his green eyes that it made me wonder if I should be afraid.

"Don't scream like that, unless you're truly in danger," he murmured in my ear before taking his hand away. "You might attract unwanted attention."

"What about attracting wanted attention?" I whispered.

I licked my lips, longing to taste him. I could feel the heat emanating from our bodies. I knew I shouldn't, but I couldn't resist any longer. I reached up and grabbed the back of his neck, pulling him towards me.

Our lips met in a fiery kiss, and it felt like the world exploded around us. His tongue danced with mine, and I moaned into his mouth, my body trembling with desire.

He pulled away slightly, his eyes dark with lust.

"We should wait," he said, his voice husky. "It's not safe here."

"I don't care," I whispered, running my hand along his pants until I felt his cock. It was hard and huge and straining against his clothing. "I want you now."

Chess groaned, his eyes flickering with desire as he realized how serious I was.

"Imagine yourself with no dress at all," he instructed.

In an instant, the burlap sack disappeared, and there I was, buck naked, my body bared to him in the light of day.

His eyes roamed over my curves, and he licked his lips hungrily.

"Oh Alice . . . you're stunning," he sighed before lowering his head and taking one of my nipples into his mouth. I stifled my groan of pleasure as he sucked and nibbled on it, his fingers teasing my other one.

"Please, Chess," I begged, my hands fisting in his dark hair. "I need you inside me."

"I know you do," he said softly, grinning so seductively. "Imagine what it'll feel like when I fuck you."

I didn't need to be asked twice. I mentally stripped off his tuxedo, the buttons flying through the decaying underbrush of the forest. Then he was flipping me around and pressing me up against the tree. I gasped as I felt his cock against my skin, thick and hot, and I spread my legs, arching my back as I offered myself to him. I imagined him rubbing his cock up and down against my wet folds, teasing me mercilessly.

He slipped one hand around to my front and massaged my clit with his fingers. I cried out in pleasure, my body arching towards him. Then, he grabbed my hips and thrust into me hard, filling me completely.

I gripped the tree with one hand, trying to keep myself upright as he pounded into me. His thrusts were hard and relentless, his hands never leaving my hips. Too soon, my pussy began to tighten around him, and I cried out as I felt myself falling over the edge.

"Oh fuck," I hissed, my whole body trembling as the orgasm swept over me. He continued to thrust into me, drawing out my euphoria as I bucked against him. Finally, he lowered his head and bit down on my shoulder, muffling his own cry of pleasure into my skin.

He stayed like that for a moment, his body still buried deep inside mine. Then he pulled out of me, and I spun around to face him.

To my absolute shock and amazement, he was completely dressed. Not one hair was out of place.

He'd never fucked me at all.

"What the hell just happened?" I gasped.

A wide grin spread across his fascinated face.

"I believe you just gave yourself one astounding orgasm. Feel better?"

"Yeah," I panted in utter confusion. "You seriously didn't fuck me just now?"

Wearing an amused grin, he slowly shook his head from side to side.

"When I fuck you, it's going to last a *lot* longer than that. And you're going to come harder than that.

And then you're going to come again, and again, and again . . . until you tell me to stop."

My belly clenched at the thought, and he must've seen the look of disbelief on my face, because he added, "All I did was play with your breasts, which are exquisite, by the way. The rest was all your doing."

He snickered under his breath, still gazing at the post-orgasm flush that was fading from my body.

"At least now we have an idea of how powerful your imagination truly is. I can't say I'm terribly surprised. Sex is where so many of our wildest fantasies reside. We can play more later, if you like, but we really ought to cover some more distance before it gets dark."

"Sure," I said, still bewildered but recovering quickly. I fanned my neck, wishing I had a scrunchie to put my hair up.

And then suddenly I was holding one.

Chess gave me a knowing smile as I twisted my hair into a messy bun.

"Ready for clothes? I certainly wouldn't mind if you chose to leave them off."

"I'm sure you wouldn't, but it doesn't seem very practical," I reasoned. With some focused thought, I was back in my blue dress and jacket, with the boots that Chess had made for me.

"Hey," I said suddenly, stopping in my tracks. "Can I ask you something?"

"Of course," he replied, his eyes locked onto mine.

"Is this really happening? Or am I just dreaming?"

I needed to know if this was all in my head, or if it was actually real.

"Does it matter?" Chess asked, smirking. "You're here, aren't you?"

"Yeah," I admitted, glancing around at the surreal forest surrounding us. "But it feels too good to be true."

"Life has a funny way of surprising us, Alice," he said, drawing closer. His hand curled around my waist, sending sparks up my back and down my legs. "Sometimes, we find what we've been searching for in the most unexpected places."

I looked into his eyes, which seemed to hold a universe of secrets, and felt an undeniable pull towards him.

"And what is it that *you've* been searching for?" I asked, my voice barely above a whisper.

"An end to Wonderland's suffering," he replied without a moment's hesitation. "Freedom from the Red Queen's reign of terror. And perhaps . . . when everything's been made right again and our world is back in balance . . . someone to share it all with. What about you, Alice? What have *you* been searching for?"

"I'm not really sure," I murmured, my heart pounding in my ears. I had thoughts on that, but every single one of them felt totally cliche and unattainable.

What was I searching for?

Loyal friends. Not people who were only nice to me until they got whatever they wanted and then bailed. Not people who were only interested in my connections, or made everything about them. I wanted badass, thoughtful, ride-or-die friends.

A higher purpose. Not like in a religious sense, but something more meaningful than a life of sleeping in until noon, then partying and shopping my life away. It might be nice to have some kind of legacy . . . or to at least have a useful, positive impact on the world.

Respect. That was a tall order, especially after my shoe empire had crashed and burned in front of the entire world. Even before that, every bad life choice I'd ever made had been documented on my family's reality TV show. Chicks like me weren't getting invitations to royal weddings. We were getting the front page of tabloids for flashing our panties while falling out of a Lamborghini.

I speak from experience.

So as I thought about Chess's loaded question, I told him the only thing I was comfortable saying out loud.

"I guess right now, all I'm searching for is that magic sword."

"Well, then, let's keep going," he said, letting go of my waist, and we continued on our journey into the heart of the unknown.

The twisted trees loomed over us, their gnarled branches reaching out for us like greedy hands. The air was thick with an unsettling blend of arousal and dread. It was twilight now, and we had wandered into a darker, more sinister part of Wonderland. I could feel the unease creeping under my skin.

"Where are we?" I asked Chess, trying to keep the tremble out of my voice.

“We’re in a place where the magic isn’t reliable. You can feel it, can’t you?”

I nodded.

“This is where things get . . . interesting," he went on, his eyes gleaming with amusement. "Wonderland has many layers, Alice. Some are darker than others."

"Great," I muttered, not sharing his enthusiasm. I reached into my jacket pocket and pulled out the map from Callister. It looked different from how I remembered it.

The once beautiful calligraphy was now jagged and scrawled, as if written by a drunk. The landmarks had shifted, rendering the map nearly indecipherable.

"Chess, look at this," I said, holding it up for him to see. "Is it just my imagination, or did the map change?”

"Ah, yes," he mused, studying the parchment. “The magic here can be quite . . . unstable."

“No shit.” I pointed to the purple ‘X’ that marked the location of the Vorpal Sword. "You see how it’s moved to the right? It's leading us in the wrong direction!”

"Is it?" he asked. "Or perhaps the sword has been moved?"

"Un-fucking-believable," I grumbled, feeling frustration bubbling under my skin. "How are we supposed to find this stupid sword if the map keeps fucking with us?"

"Trust me, Alice," he assured me. "I know these dark corners of Wonderland better than anyone. We're going to find that sword. Sometimes the greatest discoveries are made when we're lost."

"So does that mean we're lost?"

"I'm not lost, but you are," was his cryptic reply.

"If you say so," I huffed before folding the map and stuffing it back into my pocket.

We walked slower now, taking care to step over fallen logs and slimy vines. I'd fallen behind Chess, too distracted by the strange and bizarre plants and creatures that filled this dark forest. Fireflies as big as golf balls hovered in the air, lighting the way in shades of purple, green, and orange.

A flash of pink on the ground caught my eye, and I looked down to see a pair of baby bunnies chasing each other around the base of a giant mushroom.

They were fuzzy . . . and pink.

Chess and Callister had warned me about them, but it couldn't hurt to watch them play. They seemed so out of place in this dark and twisted environment, their innocence a stark contrast to the danger that lurked around every corner.

Plus, they were so damn cute.

I watched as they hopped and wrestled and

tumbled before breaking apart and looking up at me. They had huge, adorable eyes that drew me in. All I could think about was petting it and cuddling and snuggling it against my cheek.

One of the bunnies hopped over to me, stretching out its tiny pink nose as its ears swiveled in my direction. It was practically begging to be pet.

I knelt down and reached out my hand, and it nuzzled its head against my palm, sending warm fuzzies all through my body. Then the second baby bunny hopped over, wanting the same thing. Then a third bunny appeared, this one a bit bigger, but just as adorable.

"Callister was so full of shit," I said with a grin as I stroked their chinchilla-soft fur. "Look at you guys! You're the cutest little things I've ever seen!"

That's when everything went horribly wrong.

In a flash of pink, I was suddenly covered in a swarm of bunnies, all of them biting me at once with razor-sharp teeth. Pain seared through me and I started to run, screaming in terror as I tried to shake them off of me. Every time I flung one of them to the ground, it leapt back onto me and started biting even more tiny chunks of my clothes and skin.

"Chess!" I yelled as I punched a bunny away from my face. "Help!"

My heart pounded as I watched Chess's body contort and twist, his handsome features giving way to the sleek, ebony fur of a black leopard. His brilliant green eyes remained the same, glowing with a fierce intensity as he readied himself for the attack.

In a blur of black fur, he launched himself at the horde of bunnies, an explosion of fangs and claws that tore through them like tissue paper.

His powerful swipe slashed through half a dozen of them at once, rending them into bloody chunks of ears, paws, and pink fur. The sickening sound of flesh being ripped open and the squeals of the bunnies filled the air as he unleashed his wrath upon them.

I watched in both revulsion and awe as my Cheshire Cat tore into the little pink motherfuckers, his powerful jaws snapping shut around their necks, crushing bone and tearing through muscle with each bite.

Blood sprayed all over the ground in a crimson rain, staining his dark fur as he continued his relentless assault on the twisted abominations.

As quickly as it had begun, the massacre was over. The remaining bunnies let go of me and fled in terror, their fluffy tails disappearing into the twisted darkness of into the forest.

I stared in shock as I watched the black leopard gracefully rise up and slowly transform into Chess's human form, his tiger striped suit still pristine—even though he'd just brutally fought a horde of killer bunnies. I hadn't expected such a display of power, and yet there was something unsettling about it.

He seemed so composed, so detached from the carnage he had caused. It made me wonder what other hidden powers Chess had.

"Oh, Alice." he winced as he approached me and looked me up and down. The look of genuine concern in his eyes cut me to the core. "They really did a number on you. Let's find a place to stop for the night so I can take care of you."

Lifting me into his arms, he carried me into the dark, festering forest. The stench of decay hung heavily in the air, and the land itself seemed to moan in agony, as if begging for release from the torture inflicted upon it.

Chess brought me to a small clearing sheltered by towering evergreens dripping with mold and thickets of black ferns. As I rested my head against his powerful shoulder, I watched in amazement as he constructed a small, cozy cottage out of thin air.

The warm, golden light that shone from the windows was like an oasis amongst the dark trees. And even though I'd never seen this house before, I knew I'd be safe, because Chess was by my side.

CHAPTER FIVE

ALICE

"Let's get you cleaned up," Chess said softly, carrying me inside the little cottage he'd just built. A fire crackled in the hearth, casting soft shadows on the walls, and a table for two was set off to one side. He sat down on the bed, where he gently stripped me down to my panties, revealing the bites and scratches that marred my body. The sight of my injuries seemed to ignite something within him, a mix of anger and protectiveness.

"Stay still," he murmured as he knelt before me, his fingers glowing with a soft, healing light. He traced them over each bite on my arms and legs and chest, the pain fading away like a distant memory as his magic worked its wonders. I couldn't help but shiver at the sensation of his touch, my body reacting to the closeness of this enigmatic demon who had just saved my life.

"I'm sorry," I whispered, feeling tears of shame

burning my eyes. "You and Callister warned me about the bunnies, and I fucked up the second I saw them. I can't do this. I don't have what it takes to help you. Even if we find this magic sword, I'll probably fuck up again."

"Fucking up is how we learn, Alice," he said softly, pulling me into his embrace. His warmth surrounded me, providing a small comfort. "Listen to me carefully. This place is designed to break you, to test your limits. You're stronger than you think."

"No, I'm not," I said, wiping the tears off my cheeks. "I can't read a fucking map, and I almost got myself killed by piranha bunnies."

"But you were smart enough to ask for help," he pointed out while tucking a strand of hair behind my ear. "And you fought like hell against those bunnies. Your injuries aren't too bad, to be honest. Does your body hurt anywhere else?"

"I don't think so," I whispered, my voice still shaky but more determined than before.

"Are you sure about that?" he asked, his eyes darkening with desire as he looked up the length of my nearly naked body. "No pains? No aches of any kind?"

Just then, a dull, throbbing ache spread through my core, and I shuddered as I watched something shift in his expression.

Chess's gaze grew heated, dark, and intense, as if a smoldering fire had been burning deep within him all this time, and I was only seeing it now. He leaned in closer, our breaths mingling in the small space between us.

"Shall I make it better?" he asked, and I nodded. Before I knew it, his lips met mine in a searing, passionate kiss.

His mouth was hot and demanding, his tongue probing the depths of my mouth as if searching for some hidden treasure. My body responded without hesitation, melting into his embrace as if we were two pieces of a puzzle that had finally clicked together. The taste of him, a mix of sin and temptation, flooded my senses, driving all thoughts of fear and frustration from my mind.

As the kiss deepened, Chess's fingers traced a tantalizing path up my thigh until they found the lacy edge of my panties. He teased the fabric, tugging it gently before slipping his hand underneath to stroke my slick, aching folds. I moaned into his mouth, my hips bucking involuntarily at the delicious contact.

"A cat always wants the cream, Alice," he purred in my ear as he pushed his body between my knees. Still kneeling in front of me while I sat on the edge of the bed, he took off his jacket and shirt, then set them aside. "Spread your legs and let me taste you."

"Shouldn't I take these off?" I asked, teasing my finger along the embroidered words that said, 'Eat Me.' Chess shook his head and grinned.

"Not yet."

He grabbed behind my knees and pulled my ass

closer to the edge of the bed, then pushed me back against the soft cushions of the bed. I tilted my hips upwards, revealing the wet spot on my pale pink panties. With feline grace, Chess crawled slowly down between my legs, pushing them further and further apart until his warm breath fell on my delicate skin.

He nestled his head between my thighs, breathing in the sweet nectar of my arousal that pooled beneath him. He began lapping at the soft, wet fabric until it was soaked. Then he grazed his teeth over my clit until I was grinding against his face.

Chess pulled my panties to one side, exposing my slick pussy. He hungrily tasted my flesh before dipping down to let his tongue explore my depths.

I felt a long, warm, fleshy muscle probing my wet sex, searching my depths. It was thick and long, moving like a snake with a mind of its own. His tongue grew longer and thicker, filling my pussy as the wet muscle slowly thrust in and out of me.

"How the fuck are you doing that?" I gasped in wonder. Chess lifted his head, reeling his inhumanly long tongue back into his mouth.

"Alice, darling, I'm a demon," he said as his wet grin spread wide across his handsome face. "I was fucking you with my tongue. Do you like getting fucked by it, or do you only want me to lick you?"

“Oh, you can do both," I panted in delirious disbelief.

Chess gave my clit another flick, then sat up on his knees. I watched wide-eyed as he teased my wet panties down the length of my legs, over my feet, and brought them to his nose.

"Delicious," he sighed before stuffing them into his pocket. Then he crept back into position and pushed my legs wide open, leaving me exposed and vulnerable before his hungry gaze.

With fingers like cold, hard claws on my tender skin, he spread my outer lips, teasing me with soft licks and gentle sucking kisses. I wanted to come so bad. My hands sought out his unruly dark hair, tugging him further inside of me.

His hot, thick demon tongue was probing on a quest to discover my deepest pleasure. It pushed deeper into me, swelling thick and fat as it gently filled my tight walls to the brim. My hands tangled in his hair, urging him on as he fucked me with that incredible organ, each thrust more powerful than a mortal man could ever hope to achieve.

I felt an overwhelming sensation as his demon tongue fucked me and filled me again and again. It sent waves of ecstasy through my body, making me moan in delight. The texture was soft but firm against my flesh as he bathed me in teasing, relentless strokes.

My thighs began to quiver and clench as my orgasm pushed its way to the surface, but he held them in place, making his tongue vibrate as my pussy convulsed all around it.

I must've come so hard I blacked out for a second, because when I opened my eyes, Chess was lying shirtless on the bed beside me.

He rolled onto his back, then beckoned me with a finger to come closer.

"Ride my face, Alice," he taunted. "Ride my face like a fucking hobby horse."

"How did you know . . . " I panted, but he merely shook his head, then curled that finger at me one more time.

He might not ask a third, so I climbed onto him and straddled his face, pushing my wet gash against his insatiable tongue.

His probing, prehensile organ explored my depths, sending more waves of pleasure through my body. I rocked back and forth, fucking and getting fucked. I tossed my head, relishing the sensation of that slick, thick muscle rubbing up against every inch of my inner walls. I moaned his name as he licked and sucked at my clit, teasing it until it was just about ready to burst from all the pressure.

Finally I threw back my head in ecstasy as I felt Chess' demon tongue drive deeper and harder into my quivering flesh. He grasped my hips tightly in his hands, guiding my movements as I rode him like a wild beast. The sensations were overwhelming; each thrust sending a fresh wave of euphoria coursing through my core.

I let out a loud cry of pleasure as I came hard on Chess's tongue. My hands grasped the headboard as I fell forward over him in exhaustion. While I fought to catch my ragged breath, he lapped up every last drop of my juices before pulling me down to lie beside him.

I lay there speechless for a few moments before finally finding the strength to speak again.

"That was . . . incredible," I gasped, still trying to catch my breath. "My mind is . . . officially blown."

"You speak as if I'm finished with you," he said wryly as he pulled me close. "But I'm not done yet."

The moment his tongue touched me, I knew I was done for. All my thoughts melted away until I was simply a collection of nerve endings made only to feel pleasure. Chess was like nothing I'd ever experienced before–thick and sinuous, yet capable of flickering with such speed and precision that he sent me spiraling towards the edge of ecstasy within moments. He delved deeper, his tongue flexing and stretching me in ways that felt both alien and amazing.

"Chess . . . oh, god!" I cried out, my body writhing beneath his skilled touch. It was too much–and yet, not enough.

The wet, slick sound of his tongue plunging into me filled the air, mingling with my desperate gasps and moans. My body tensed, teetering on the edge of an orgasm so intense I was sure it would tear me apart.

Just when I thought I couldn't take any more, Chess redoubled his efforts, pressing his thumb against my swollen clit while his tongue plunged even deeper inside me.

"Come again for me, Alice," he growled, the vibrations of his voice sending me hurtling over the edge.

My climax ripped through me like a wildfire,

leaving me breathless and shaking in its wake. Still trembling from the intense pleasure, I looked up at Chess, my eyes pleading with him.

"I want you inside me," I whispered, my voice shaky and raw.

"I've *been* inside you," he pointed out. I shook my head in frustration.

"No, not with your tongue," I moaned while reaching for his crotch. "I want something stiffer. Something harder. I want you to fuck me!"

He hesitated, his expression clouded with concern.

"Alice, I . . . I can't," he said softly, his hand gently stroking my hair.

"What do you mean?" I howled in frustration. "You're as hard as a fucking rock!"

"Oh, I'm well aware, but if I were to get carried away, it would use up too much of my magic powers. I need to be able to protect you."

"Damn it," I panted, my chest heaving as I struggled to control the overwhelming waves of lust crashing over me. The disappointment was a bitter taste on my tongue, but I knew Chess was right. His magic had been the only thing keeping me safe from the twisted creatures of Wonderland.

But as much as I couldn't risk him losing that power just for my own selfish desires, there was a part of me that was already planning to try.

I'd seduce him one way or the other.

"The minute it's safe, I want you to fuck me

senseless," I finally sighed, my body still shaking from how much I wanted him.

"Consider that a promise," he replied with a wicked grin, his green eyes glinting in the dim light of our enchanted cottage. He leaned down to press a soft kiss to my lips, the taste of my arousal still lingering on his tongue. I moaned into the kiss, feeling a mixture of frustration and anticipation.

"Until then," he murmured against my lips, "I'll do everything in my power to make sure you're satisfied."

"Good," I huffed, trying to regain some semblance of control over my body. "Because if you don't, I might go insane."

"Going mad in Wonderland? We wouldn't want that now, would we?" Chess teased. He brushed a stray lock of my blonde hair away from my face before leaning down to capture my lips once more, his kiss delicious, yet leaving me wanting more.

So much more.

I didn't like being teased.

After showering and having breakfast the next morning, we left our magical cottage, which evaporated into a fine mist the second we walked out the door. Chess refused to give me back my panties, and I wasn't able to imagine new ones for myself.

I reached into my pocket and took out the map.

For one long, confusing moment I wasn't even sure it was the same one that Callister had given me. The calligraphy looked like someone had made a crude attempt at writing with a crayon. The purple 'X' was barely more than a splash of watercolor dried on the page. The landmarks were scribbled randomly as if nothing more than a drunken sketch.

"This map is next to useless!"

"Seeing as how you're next to the map, are you suggesting that you're useless?" Chess teased. I glared at him so hard that I half expected bolts of fire to come shooting out of my eyes. Chess didn't back down at all. In fact, I think he liked seeing me so frustrated.

"Look at it for yourself," I growled through gritted teeth. "This fucking map is leading us all over the place! I think Callister did this on purpose! Why would he sabotage us like this?"

"I don't know if it was intentional, but he certainly has a way of complicating things." Chess's green eyes flickered with uncertainty, his constant grin briefly fading. He signed, running a hand through his tousled black hair. "He has a difficult time trusting others. I imagine he's testing you."

"Testing me? Why?"

"Well . . . " Chess began, "he's probably curious to see how committed you truly are to saving Wonderland."

"That shady asshole! I'm here, aren't I?"

I tossed my long blonde hair over my shoulder,

reminding myself not to scream, even though it was all I wanted to do. I couldn't believe how much time we'd wasted because of that manipulative bastard.

"What are we going to do now?" I asked, my voice breaking slightly. "We can't keep wandering around aimlessly like this. Do you have any helpful suggestions on how to find this stupid sword?"

"We could ask the Mad Hatter where it is," Chess replied with a little shrug. "After all, he's the one who had the Vorpal Sword last."

My eyes flashed in outrage.

"He knows where it is?" I screeched. "Why didn't you say so in the first place?"

"It was the very first thing I said." His mouth twisted into a little smirk. "I simply didn't think to say it out loud."

"Alright, well, from now on, you'd better stop saying things in your head and start saying them out loud. Got it?"

"Got what?"

"Did you understand what I said?" I seethed, which only made Chess grin wider.

"You want me to stop keeping my thoughts to myself and start saying them out loud? Is that correct?"

"Yes!" I cried, throwing my hands up in frustration. "I don't think that's asking very much."

"I don't think you realize what you're asking at all. Some of my thoughts are quite depraved."

"I don't care!" I said, shoving the map back into

my jacket pocket as I stomped along the path. "I'm from LA! I've seen and heard it all! There's not a fucking thing you could say or do that would shock me."

Chess's Cheshire Cat grin spread wide across his sensual mouth.

"Well, I know that's not true, but I'll play along for now."

I walked for a few more seconds, until I stopped in my tracks.

"Am I even headed in the right direction?"

Still grinning, Chess shook his head and hooked his thumb over his shoulder.

"I should've known," I groaned. "What's down is up, and what's up is down, right?"

Chess's grin spread even wider across his handsome face. I would've slapped him if it weren't for that amazing demon tongue of his.

"See? You're starting to figure things out already."

We walked for a few moments before I looked up at him.

"Why didn't you tell me out loud that the Mad Hatter knew where the sword was all along?"

"Because the chances of the Mad Hatter being lucid enough to remember its location are slim to none. Hatter was once a loyal servant of the White Queen. When it became clear that you weren't coming to save us, she asked him to steal the sword from the Red Queen. The White Queen is so merciful and kind that she wanted to protect not just her Kingdom of Diamonds and Ice, but also her sister's Kingdom of Hearts and Roses. She wanted to keep all of Wonderland from the Red Queen's wicked grasp, and Hatter was happy to help her."

"He sounds very loyal to her," I remarked.

Chess gave me a sympathetic look.

"He is. Unfortunately, the power of the sword proved too much for his mind, and he succumbed to madness. He hid the sword to keep it from driving him even further into madness. And even if he *did* remember where it was, there's no guarantee he'd be willing to share that knowledge with us."

"Wouldn't he tell *me*?" I asked as we walked further into the decaying forest. "After all, I'm the one who's supposed to use it."

"His mind is a labyrinth of madness and riddles," Chess replied, his expression darkening. "He may be our only hope of finding the sword, but he's not one to be trifled with. He won't hesitate to fuck you over. He'll probably do it right over the table."

"I'd like to see him fucking try," I laughed.

Chess hesitated, eyeing hungrily me from head to toe. Then he leaned closer, his breath hot on my ear.

"You must be careful what you ask for, Alice. Hatter is known for his . . . insatiable appetite."

Insatiable appetite?

That sure as hell got my attention. My ears perked up the second I heard those words, and I felt an ache deep inside. An ache that made my stomach coil with both anticipation and need. An ache that wouldn't have been there if Chess would've simply fucked me like I'd begged him to earlier.

"I honestly don't even care at this point," I said firmly, my heart pounding wildly in my chest. "We need that sword, Chess. And if the Mad Hatter can help us find it, then I'll deal with whatever he has in store."

CHAPTER SIX

CALLISTER

I took a drag from the hookah sitting near me, the dark pink smoke curling around me like a lover's embrace. The table laid out in front of me resembled a hallucinogenic wet dream, with teacups that seemed to breathe and cakes that oozed thick, pulsating syrup.

The towering mansion in front of me cast shadows that danced across the trees that surrounded the garden, making eerie patterns that seemed to come alive before my eyes. Teapots, teacups, and plates of magic-laced pastries floated through the air, while bright, colorful candles flickered all around an enormous table, casting a multitude of shades upon the guests.

The Mad Hatter's tea parties were widely known throughout Wonderland to be a cesspool of fuckery, but this time he'd outdone himself. A giant, contorted teapot loomed above us, pouring steaming liquid into mismatched cups that danced around his long, crooked table. The guests were an eclectic mix of demonic creatures and curious human souls who'd lost their way.

If they weren't laughing and drinking themselves senseless amidst the chaos, they were engaging in acts that would make even the most jaded libertine blush. Dormouse was passed out face down in a plate of petit fours while Harry the March Hare was plundering a shy Violet into oblivion from the comfort of his chair.

So imagine my surprise when Chess came strolling down the zigzag path that led into Hatter's back garden with Alice hanging on his arm. Half-crazed laughter echoed from all around the garden, so loud and raucous that even if Chess had bothered to announce their arrival, nobody would've heard him.

I watched as a mixture of curiosity, apprehension, and excitement spread across Alice's face when Chess's hand slipped around her waist and guided her towards Hatter, who was seated at the head of the table.

She couldn't tear her eyes away from him, and I immediately knew what she was thinking.

Hatter wasn't anything like she was expecting. He was tall, powerful, yet lean, and had one bright blue eye and one dark brown that unnerved everyone who gazed too long at his face. His chiseled features were framed by unruly locks of dark indigo hair, while his piercing eyes seemed to hold the mysteries of the universe. He wore a dark blue velvet vest and an old-fashioned cravat instead of a necktie, a lackadaisical dandy. A well-worn top hat sat on his head at a rakish angle, completing his fascinating, yet bizarre ensemble.

"Chess! How lovely it is to see you, my friend!" he said as he stood up from his chair. His intense gaze flicked from Alice's legs to her beautiful face, making a quick study before redirecting back onto Chess. "Dormouse was just asking Callister if one were to remove the wings from a butterfly, would it then become a caterpillar?"

"Preposterous!" Dormouse yawned as if it was a struggle to hold up his tired head from his pillow of plated pastries. "That's like saying if you take away the clouds, the sky would cease to exist!"

"Perhaps the sky is merely hiding," I said dryly, my cigarette bobbing in between my lips as I spoke. "I'm surprised you made it this far, Alice."

"Alice?" Hatter mused, his eyes burning with a spark of unbridled lust. I knew in that instant that my mad friend would make it his mission to fuck her.

Alice stared wide-eyed at the surreal spectacle before her, her luscious pink lips spreading apart as her jaw fell open. My cock twitched as I thought about shoving it into her soft, warm, wet mouth.

Patience, I told myself. If she hadn't already fucked Chess, I was sure she would soon. But I didn't want her now. Not when she was still new to Wonderland and full of hope.

No, I wanted her once she was broken by our wicked, warped realm. Once Chess had had his fill.

Once Hatter had fucked her so hard he'd left her aching and raw.

I wanted her used.

Secondhand.

Thirdhand.

Her long blonde hair cascaded down her blue dress and caught on her incredible tits, making me wonder how much further down the rabbit hole Alice would fall.

Her body tensed, no doubt overwhelmed by the strange and surreal atmosphere.

"Yes, she's finally arrived in Wonderland," Chess replied. "Alice, these are my friends Hatter, Dormouse, and Harry the March Hare."

Harry's eyes darted over to Alice briefly as he kept fucking Violet.

"You already know Callister. Everyone, this is Alice."

"Nice to meet you," she said, giving us a timid little wave.

"Oh, the pleasure is all mine," Hatter said, taking her hand in his. With a playful grin, he gave it a soft kiss before letting it go. "Do join us, my dear! There's always room for more madness at this table . . . especially if you come sit beside me."

Alice hesitated for a moment, glancing at Chess for reassurance. Her delicate eyebrows were furrowed in concern.

"You told me to be careful of what I eat or drink while I'm here."

Chess quirked a curious brow at her, amusement dancing in his green eyes.

"That depends. How bad do you want to find that sword?"

I watched Alice take a deep breath. With determination etched on her beautiful face, she strode over to the table and took the seat closest to Hatter, which he'd pulled out for her in an effort to appear chivalrous.

If only she knew the truth about him.

But if I knew Hatter, then Alice was going to find out about him soon enough.

As Alice scooted her chair closer to the table, I could see the gears turning in her head. Our world was unlike anything she had ever known, and she was desperate to find her place in it.

Meanwhile, Chess curled up in the chair between her and myself. I could tell by the way he licked his lips that he'd already tasted her.

"Marvelous," crooned the Mad Hatter as Alice sank her pert round ass into the chair next to him. "Let the festivities continue. Alice, would you care for any tea?" Hatter was already pouring her a steaming cup from a teapot that seemed to change colors as it moved. "It'll help you see things more clearly."

Again, she turned to Chess for approval.

Chess gave her a nod and a sly grin, encouraging her to accept the strange offering. Tentatively, she took a sip, her pink lips wrapping around the edge of the cup, her eyes widening as the peculiar liquid slid down her throat.

"Interesting," she murmured, taking another sip.

"Ah, there's that adventurous spirit I knew you had in you!" the Mad Hatter snickered while clapping his hands together.

"Let's see how good you are at riddles. We've been telling them all night."

"Okay," Alice said, appearing more comfortable with her surroundings.

"What is incredibly hard and fits into a tiny hole?"

A red flush crept over Alice's face, yet Hatter didn't even flinch. He simply grinned in satisfaction.

"A key!" said Dormouse.

"You are correct," Hatter declared. "What about this one? What's the difference between 'ooooooh' and 'aaaaaaah'?"

"About three inches!" Violet moaned, still bouncing on Harry the March Hare's lap. A round of laughter rose up from the table.

"You would know," Hatter said. Alice was finding it hard to look away from the copulating couple, but she forced herself to stare at her host's face as he offered another riddle.

"I have a long, stiff shaft. My tip penetrates. I come with a quiver. What am I? Alice, do you know what I am?"

Bless her, she bit down on her bottom lip and all I knew Hatter was already planning on how to penetrate her with his long, stiff shaft.

"A dick?" she suggested.

Hatter shook his head, then glanced around the table.

Nobody had an answer for him.

"I have a long, stiff shaft," he repeated. "My tip penetrates. I come with a quiver. What am I?"

"I don't know," Alice admitted with a sad little shrug.

"Then you must think hard and long on the matter," said Hatter, before clinking his teacup against hers. "When you figure it out, do let me know."

"I will."

"What do you think about our mad little tea party?"

"There's nothing little about it," I said under my breath so only Chess could hear me. I heard him laugh to himself. Then we watched as Alice's pupils dilated and a flush spread across her cheeks. The room seemed to shimmer and distort around us, as if we were watching her watching Wonderland through a kaleidoscope.

All around us, the party guests continued with their twisted games, their raucous laughter mixing with moans and gasps of pleasure. As Alice's senses sharpened, I watched as she became more aware of the debauchery surrounding her, and I could tell by the way she squirmed in her chair that both curiosity and arousal stirred within her.

"Chess," she said, her voice barely audible over the cacophony of the party. "I want to try some of the food, but . . . I'm afraid of what will happen."

"Relax, darling. Fear is just another form of excitement," Chess replied, running a hand through her hair. "And here, in this world, fear and desire go hand in hand. Trust me, Alice. Trust Hatter. He's an old friend of mine, and he won't let any harm come to you. We'll guide you through the chaos."

"That's right, Alice," Hatter said, grinning seductively at her. "Embrace the madness."

His words seemed to soothe her somewhat, and she hesitantly reached for a delectable cupcake sitting on a tall, tiered tray in front of her. I couldn't help but smirk as I watched her trying to make sense of it all. It was about time someone shook up her pampered life.

Then her little wet, pink tongue slid out of her mouth, licking at the soft white frosting. Finally she sank her teeth into it, filling her mouth with the sweetness. A need to dominate her took hold of me, and I couldn't help but feel a pang of envy to be that chocolate cupcake. In about thirty seconds, she was going to be hot and flushed and wanting to either fight . . .

. . . or fuck.

When the magic kicked in, it looked like she wanted to do both.

My kind of woman.

Damn it, she was something else—a mix of innocence and depravity that I found almost impossible to resist.

But for now, I'd have to bide my time and watch as she navigated the twisted Wonderland we called home. And who knew, maybe one day soon, I'd get a taste of Alice myself.

I watched as she stared wide-eyed at the surreal scene before her, a mixture of fascination and terror painted across her beautiful face. The tea party was in full swing, a cacophony of moans, laughter, and the clinking of porcelain cups filling the air.

"Feeling out of your depth, Alice?" I asked, taking a drag from my cigarette and letting the fruity pink smoke curl around me. "Afraid you don't have what it takes to survive here?"

Her eyes narrowed, and I could see the fire of defiance flicker within them. "I'm not afraid," she spat back, though I knew better.

"Really? You can hardly handle this little tea party. How will you manage when the real fuckery begins?" I taunted, smirking at her mounting frustration.

"Callister," Chess scolded, but I ignored him. He was too busy playing the protective friend.

"You're allowing yourself to remain blind to the fact that Alice needs to be pushed if she's going to discover her true potential," I countered. "Have you even bothered to see what she's capable of?"

"We're working on it," Chess answered, yet I could tell I'd hit a nerve. That pleasure-seeking feline demon was probably too busy trying to seduce Alice to bother teaching her how to use the Vorpal Sword . . . if she ever found it.

"Show me what you can do," Hatter said before Chess and I could start bickering. Harry the March

Hare even stopped fucking Violet long enough to watch as Alice's bright blue dress melted into purple, and then red.

Hatter's eyes, wild with crazed curiosity, locked onto her.

"Charming as that trick is, my dear, it's clear you have *much* to learn. The good news is that I believe you have more power within you than you realize. Allow me to help you embrace the darker side of your imagination."

Alice hesitated, glancing between Chess and Hatter, uncertainty etched on her features. She bit her lip, considering his offer, and I couldn't deny the surge of jealousy that coursed through me at the thought of her accepting his guidance.

It was Chess who broke the silence, his voice as smooth and seductive as ever. "Go on, Alice," he urged her, his green eyes flickering with something akin to excitement. "The Mad Hatter's offer is a rare one. I believe it will help you find your purpose here in Wonderland."

"Fine," Alice said finally, her voice wavering only slightly. "I'll do it." The Mad Hatter clapped his hands together gleefully, his attraction to Alice palpable. Even amidst all the madness, it was obvious that he desired her.

"Excellent!" he exclaimed, jumping up from his seat at the head of the table. "Let's begin right away! You can be our entertainment!"

As Chess joined Alice and the Mad Hatter, I couldn't help but feel a sting of jealousy. She was so eager to please them both, and so eager to irritate me.

For now, I resigned myself to watching from the sidelines, focusing on the smoke from my magic cigarette as it twisted into intricate patterns.

"First," the Mad Hatter announced, "we must teach you how to manipulate your surroundings. Observe!" With a wave of his hand, he conjured a small teapot that floated gracefully in mid-air. Alice stared at it, wide-eyed, as if she'd just witnessed the impossible.

"Now, you try," Chess prompted, his voice low and encouraging. "Focus on something simple and imagine it coming to life."

Alice took a deep breath, her brow furrowed in concentration. Slowly, hesitantly, she raised her hand, her fingers trembling ever so slightly. And then, before our very eyes, the sugar bowl on the table began to float upwards, its contents swirling around like a miniature tornado. She gasped, a mixture of shock and delight written across her face.

"Amazing!" the Mad Hatter exclaimed, clapping his hands together. "You're a natural, my dear."

"See, Alice?" Chess said with a smirk. "I knew you had it in you."

"Beginner's luck," I muttered under my breath, though I couldn't help but be impressed by her progress. I steeled myself as I watched Alice trying to keep up with the peculiarities of it all.

Emboldened by her success, she continued to practice, her powers growing stronger and more refined with each passing moment. She conjured teacups that danced in mid-air, their fragile porcelain bodies twirling gracefully like ballerinas.

A procession of cakes materialized out of thin air, each more delectable and decadent than the last. Even the table itself seemed to come alive, its wooden surface undulating like waves on a stormy sea.

As the other guests marveled at her creations, laughing and cheering as they drank tea and devoured cake, I found myself begrudgingly captivated by Alice's newfound abilities. She was not only surviving in this twisted Wonderland—she was *thriving*, embracing her newly discovered powers with a sense of wonder and determination.

"Watch closely, Alice," the Mad Hatter instructed as he waved his arms about in a flourish. An intricate puzzle of gears and cogs appeared before our eyes, interlocking and spinning in a mesmerizing dance.

"Go on, give it a try," Chess encouraged, giving Alice a playful nudge.

"Alright," she said, squaring her shoulders and narrowing her eyes in concentration. With a flick of her delicate wrist, Alice manipulated the gears, making them spin faster and more fluidly than before. The air around her seemed to crackle with energy, and I couldn't help but feel the hair on the back of my neck lift up in anticipation of whatever might come next.

"Very impressive," I admitted grudgingly, my tone dripping with sarcasm. "You've learned the most basic control of magic. Congratulations."

"Thank you, Callister," she replied sweetly, though her eyes flashed with mischief. "Let's see what else I can come up with."

With that declaration, Alice began to unleash a torrent of imaginative creations that left the tea party guests gasping in awe. Wine glasses filled with thick red liquid sprouted from twisted vines, each glass accompanied by the intoxicating scent of roses. Gossamer-winged butterflies fluttered through the air, their wings adorned with intricate patterns of gold and silver.

"Enough with the pretty shit, Alice," I sneered, masking my growing admiration for her abilities. "What can you do that's actually useful?"

"Useful?" she echoed, raising an eyebrow. "What's wrong, Callister? Don't you think pretty things can be useful?"

"Beauty doesn't get you far in Wonderland," I replied, my voice low.

"Fine," Alice snapped, her eyes narrowing with determination. She took a deep breath, and as she exhaled, she summoned a menagerie of grotesque creatures, their twisted forms a stark contrast to the delicate beauty of her previous creations.

"Is this more to your liking, Callister?" she asked, a wicked grin playing at the corners of her lips. "Or do you need something more . . . explicit?"

I couldn't help but grin at her audacity. This pampered party girl from Los Angeles had some bite to her after all. I took a drag from my hookah, the raspberry smoke swirling around me as I exhaled.

"Alright, Alice," I conceded, nodding towards her monstrous creations. "You've got my attention. Show me what else you can do."

"Only if you promise not to be such an insufferable prick," she retorted, her eyes narrowing into slits.

"I'll try," I grumbled, rolling my eyes. "But only because I'm curious about the extent of your abilities."

"Deal," she replied with a prim smile, and with that truce in place, we continued to watch as Alice pushed the boundaries of her powers, bending the magic of Wonderland to her whims in ways I'd never seen before.

And as much as it pained me to admit it, I found myself becoming increasingly intrigued by this infuriating, intoxicating woman who had stumbled into our twisted realm.

"Hey, Callister," Alice taunted, her voice dripping with sarcasm. "How about a friendly little duel to see just how far my powers have come? Or are you afraid of having your ass kicked by a girl?"

"Oh, you can fuck right off," I growled, although I couldn't help the wicked gleam that filled my eyes at the thought of battling this infuriating woman.

"Come on, Callister," she continued, her grin growing wider as she saw the interest flicker in my eyes. "Afraid I'll make you look bad?"

"More like I'm afraid I'll make you sorry you challenged me," I said, setting aside my hookah. I quickly summoned a twisted sword made of shadows and blue smoke, grinning wide when she realized what she was dealing with.

"Let's see what you've got, princess."

"Finally, some excitement!" cackled Hatter, clapping his hands together in anticipation. He motioned for the other guests to clear a space, and they eagerly complied, forming a circle around Alice and me. Whispers and bets flew through the crowd, their excitement palpable. Even Harry had given up on trying to fuck Violet to completion.

"Ready when you are, honey," Alice smirked, conjuring a blade of pure ice that shimmered dangerously in the dim light.

"Try not to cry too hard when you lose, sweetheart," I retorted, lunging forward with my shadowy weapon.

Our blades clashed, filling the air with the sound of cracking ice and the hiss of dissipating smoke. Alice parried my strikes with surprising skill, her eyes never leaving mine as we danced our deadly waltz. The crowd cheered us on, their voices a dull roar in the background as I focused on the woman before me.

Where had she learned to fight like this? To *move* like this?

"Is that all you've got?" Alice taunted, ducking under a swing and sweeping her leg out to trip me. I stumbled but recovered quickly, gritting my teeth as I tried to anticipate her next move.

"Hardly," I shot back, slicing my sword through the air and sending a wave of darkness towards her. She countered with a blast of icy wind that cut through my attack like a knife, leaving us both unscathed.

"Interesting," I mused, my brow furrowing in concentration. "Perhaps you're not entirely useless after all."

"Thanks for the vote of confidence," she replied sarcastically, launching herself into the air and summoning a barrage of razor-sharp icicles to rain down upon me. I dodged and weaved, the chill of near misses nipping at my skin.

"Enough of this shit!" I bellowed, my frustration mounting as I wrapped tendrils of smoke around Alice's ankles, yanking her from the sky and slamming her onto the ground.

"Fuck!" she cursed, wincing as she tried to break free of my grip. But as I approached her prone form, ready to claim victory, she revealed her cunning.

With a wicked grin, Alice unleashed a torrent of ice that encased my feet, rooting me to the spot.

"Gotcha," she whispered, her breath hot against my ear as she slipped out of my grasp and stood up. She placed the tip of her ice blade against my chest, her eyes dancing with triumph. "Yield?"

"Fuck you, princess," I spat, but there was no heat behind my words. The crowd erupted in cheers and applause, their bets settled and their thirst for entertainment sated. "Where the hell did a spoiled brat like you learn to fight like that?"

"My parents made me study fencing for six years," Alice gloated from above, pressing her blade closer for emphasis. "Maybe that'll teach you to underestimate me."

"In your dreams," I growled, though deep down, I knew she had earned every ounce of respect I could muster. I couldn't help but marvel at the power and determination that radiated from her, even as the ice around my feet began to melt. Wonderland had truly changed her, and I couldn't deny that I was starting to see Alice in a new light.

"I'm already there. Let's see what else I can dream up for you," Alice declared with a smirk. Suddenly she conjured a whirlwind to encircle us, the howling winds creating a barrier between our duel and the avidly watching guests.

"Fucking shit, Alice," I muttered under my breath, begrudgingly admiring her skill. "You really are full of surprises."

"Get used to it," she retorted, her eyes flashing with fire. As the whirlwind dissipated, the crowd's cheers and applause reached a fever pitch. Some of the guests even howled in delight, their twisted faces contorted in ecstasy at the thrilling spectacle they had just witnessed. "Still think I'm useless?"

"No, I don't," I conceded, glaring at her. "But don't expect me to go easy on you next time."

"I wouldn't want you to," she replied with a flirtatious grin.

Just then, Chess appeared beside her, his green eyes shining with pride.

"Didn't I tell you?" he purred, wrapping an arm

around her waist. "I knew Alice was something special."

"And she's more imaginative than we could've hoped," Hatter chimed in, taking Alice's free hand and raising it in victory. "Congratulations, my dear! Wonderland has finally found its champion to save us from the Red Queen!"

"Thanks," Alice said, her cheeks flushing at the praise. She looked around at the assembled guests, their eyes filled with admiration and approval, and for the first time since she arrived in this fucked-up world, she looked like she belonged here.

"Drinks all around!" Hatter announced, leading us back to the tea table where fresh cups awaited us. The guests resumed their drunken debauchery, the air filled with moans of pleasure as they stuffed their faces with cake and candies. Harry the March Hare led Violet into the woods to fuck her without any more interruptions, and I loaded my hookah with coconut lime tobacco. A flick of a match and its subsequent flames danced around the bowl while I packed another pinch of tobacco into the top of the pipe.

"Drink up, Alice," Chess whispered in her ear, handing her a teacup that smelled of roses and sin. "You've earned it."

"Careful, Chess," I murmured, watching as Alice took a hearty gulp. I sucked in air through my teeth as I pushed at the tobacco, trying to draw out more of the tropical flavor. "We don't want her to lose her edge now, do we?"

"Chill out, Callister," Alice shot back, her eyes gleaming with mischief. "I can handle myself." She took another long drink and then licked her pink lips in satisfaction. "Besides, I'm starting to really like the taste."

"Of course you like the taste of sin, my dear," Hatter said, reaching under the table towards her thighs, eliciting a soft moan from her mouth. "We all do, eventually."

"Damn straight," Alice agreed, clinking her teacup against his.

I watched as Hatter whispered something into her ear that made her blush all the way from her cheeks to the perfect tits that were heaving beneath the tight confines of her dress. As much as I hated to admit it, their sickening flirtation was getting under my skin.

Chess leaned close to me, his voice dripping with playful sarcasm.

"Why Callister . . . you look like you're about to crawl out of your skin in frustration. Don't be jealous. You know Hatter and I always share everything with you."

"Why would I be jealous of that deranged lunatic?" I scoffed while taking another drag of my hookah. "I just don't know what she sees in him, that's all."

"Well," Chess mused thoughtfully, "perhaps it's because he can offer her something that you can't."

"And what the hell would that be?" I spat, my anger flaring like the bowl of my hookah.

"The true location of the Vorpal Sword," Chess replied, his voice soft and deadly serious. "I know you gave her that cursed map to throw her off course and make her give up, but just look at her . . . she's probably bargaining with Hatter to see what he wants in exchange for the right information."

"I'm pretty sure I know what he wants from her," I grumbled, taking another swig of my tea. It tasted like liquid sin, burning a path down my throat as it threatened to ignite the darkness within me. "Do you think she'll do it?"

"Perhaps," Chess conceded. "They do seem rather drawn to one another. And," he added as an afterthought, "I have been teasing her a fair bit. That's why I've kept her panties . . . they'd only get in the way. I thought she'd be satisfied with multiple tongue fuckings, but apparently all I've done is leave her wanting more."

"*More*?" I hissed, half in disbelief, and half in delight. "What a greedy little slut!"

"I know," Chess agreed with a subtle nod, his eyes never leaving Alice's flushed face as Hatter whispered depraved things in her delicate ear.

Of course Chess's demonic green eyes never left her face. That fucker loved to watch. I'd lost track of how many times I'd been fucking a girl and he'd been invisible, yet watching us the whole time.

One got used to it after living with a demon for so long.

"But for now, we should focus on celebrating the fact that Alice has been able to tap into her imagination better than either of us expected. I do believe she'll be the one to defeat the Red Queen."

As the night wore on and the debauchery reached new heights, I couldn't help but feel a twisted sense of pride in what Alice had accomplished. She might have been a pain in my ass, but there was no denying that she had talent—and guts.

"Callister," Hatter called, looking at me with a grin that would've made Chess proud. "Tell me, what do you think of our dear Alice? Do you think she's worthy of the task ahead of her?"

"It's hard to say, my friend," I replied, sucking the last of the coconut lime tobacco into my lungs. Spirals of pale green smoke drifted over the guests who were still seated at the table . . . the ones who hadn't wandered off to fuck in the bushes. "I think Alice needs to decide that for herself."

I turned my attention to the blonde he was still fingering under the table. She thought she was hiding it so well, but I knew better.

A woman didn't move and twist her body like that unless she wanted to get fucked.

"How bad you want to find that sword, princess?" I asked, sitting back in my chair. "Are you willing to do whatever it takes?"

"Yeah, I am," she said, and her pink lips morphed into a twisted, devilish grin. "Watch me."

I had no idea what she had in mind.

But I was about to find out.

CHAPTER
SEVEN
ALICE

"More tea?" the Mad Hatter inquired, his voice lilting and teasing. Entranced, I nodded, accepting a fresh teacup emblazoned with "Drink Me" and taking a long drink of the deliciousness. Another round of warmth spread through my body like liquid fire, igniting a boldness I'd never experienced before.

It was probably why I was grinding against Hatter's palm at that very moment. I'd let guys finger me in public before, but never someone I'd only met an hour ago.

That boldness was also why, when Callister looked down his nose at me and asked me how bad I wanted to find the Vorpal Sword, I came up with a plan that would show him *exactly* how serious I was.

"Watch me," I told him with a smile.

Then I turned back to Hatter.

I shuddered as I felt him moving inside my body. I was squirming and so wet that I was sure I was going to leave a wet spot on my chair.

But I didn't care.

I could imagine it away if I wanted to.

"Your party is fucking amazing," I told him, my voice breathy and flirtatious as I met his hypnotic gaze.

There was something so feral about his mismatched eyes. The brown one promised that he'd take good care of me, while the blue one suggested he'd tear me apart and leave me begging for more.

My inhibitions had completely vanished, and I found myself leaning even closer to him, entranced by the wild, untamed light that flickered behind his beautiful eyes.

"I know it's amazing," he chuckled, "but my dear Alice, you've only just arrived. Let me make you come."

"Mmmm," I hummed. "Are you sure the answer to your riddle from earlier isn't your cock?"

Slowly, ever so slowly, Hatter shook his head.

"I have a long, stiff shaft," he said, his voice full of double entendre. "My tip penetrates. I come with a quiver. What am I, Alice?"

"I honestly don't know. Can't you give me a clue?"

"I cannot. It would take away all the fun."

"Alright, then I guess you'll just have to tell me where you hid the Vorpal Sword," I sighed, my words laced with newfound confidence.

The air in the room thickened, and the Mad Hatter's eyes widened at my bold inquiry. March Hare tensed up, his jittery hands pausing mid-pour, sharing a surprised glance with the drowsy Dormouse. Chess laughed, a wicked, throaty sound that echoed through the garden.

"I'm afraid I don't remember where I put it," Hatter said with a shrug. "I can only think clearly when I'm completely relaxed, which isn't often."

"I know what would make you completely relaxed."

"Bold move," Hatter said, a slow grin of approval spreading across his face, "you're learning to embrace the madness."

"Oh, I learned how to do that a long time ago," I teased, making his eyes flash with lust.

"Shall we make an agreement in front of all these witnesses?" he suggested, his voice dark and seductive, his eyes glinting with desire. "You give me something of a certain value, and I'll give you something of equal value." He paused, letting the tension build before continuing. "An incredible fuck, right here, in exchange for me telling you where the sword is. What do you say?"

The room seemed to close in on itself as the Mad Hatter leaned forward, resting his elbows on the table, his eyes never leaving mine. I held his gaze, refusing to back down. The world around me might have been dark and twisted, but I would face it head-on, no matter the cost.

"Come on, Alice," urged Chess. "Take one for the team!"

"I don't think she'll actually do it," scoffed Callister.

My heart skipped a beat, and for a moment, I was speechless. The realization hit me that I had never encountered someone who could so effortlessly command my attention and make me question everything I thought I knew about myself. My pussy clenched so hard in excitement that I barely noticed the other guests around the table.

Even so, I didn't have to think about Hatter's offer twice.

"I say bring it on."

My tone was almost casual, revealing none of the turmoil churning inside me. To be honest, I found Hatter's enigmatic nature and striking appearance undeniably sexy, and I wanted to tap into the insanity lurking behind his eyes. I saw it as a challenge, a way to push myself beyond my comfort zone and embrace my rebellious instincts.

Hatter's lips curved into a sly grin, clearly pleased by my response. "You're a fascinating creature, Alice," he murmured, his eyes darkening with desire. "Very well. We have a deal."

To my dismay, he pulled his fingers out of me and picked up a dainty plate holding a small slice of cake smothered in bright pink frosting. Then he held it out to me.

"I made this just for you. But I want to watch you eat it without using your hands."

I hesitated for a moment, feeling the weight of Chess's gaze on me as I considered the proposition. I licked my lips, suddenly aware of the ache in my core.

With a spark of defiance, I accepted the cake and held the plate in my hands, then lowered my mouth and took a bite. The cake was tender and moist, so sweet on my lips.

Hatter sat back in his chair, studying me with delight dancing in his wild mismatched eyes as I tried not to get too much frosting on my chin.

"Good girl," the Mad Hatter murmured, his voice low and sultry.

Slowly, deliberately, I traced my tongue along the top, collecting some of the rich, sweet frosting on the tip.

As the taste filled my senses, I locked eyes with Hatter and leaned forward, giving him a stellar view of my tits. The sweetness mingled with the warmth of our shared breath, and I could feel the pulse of power between us.

"Did you enjoy that?" he asked, watching as I swiped a bit of frosting off my cheek and brought it to my lips.

"It's the best cake I've ever tasted," I admitted.

"How good is it?" he asked. "Good enough to lick the plate clean?"

"Yeah."

"Then do it," he ordered. "I want to see what your little pink tongue is capable of."

Obediently, I lifted the plate and began to lick off the frosting with long, broad strokes. The tip of my tongue danced along the edge of the cold porcelain, dissolving the bright pink frosting until it melted in my mouth.

Hatter's eyes narrowed as he sucked in a breath. His cock stirred awake and began to swell in his striped pants until finally he couldn't stand it anymore.

"Come over here," he murmured, gently grabbing my hand and pulling me onto his lap. He wrapped his arms around my waist as I straddled him. He brought me closer to him and tasted the frosting from my lips before pressing a passionate kiss against them. His hands explored my body as we kissed, sliding down, then underneath my dress to grab my bare ass in his strong hands.

"Are you still wet for me?"

I grinned and nodded my head.

"Good girl."

There was a brief moment as he took out his cock, and then he pressed the length between my lips. I slid up and down his shaft, rubbing my clit against the head of his cock, kissing him until I didn't know where the frosting ended and his tongue began.

After begging repeatedly for Chess's dick and being turned down, I was more than ready for Hatter to fuck me. The friction against my clit was building, but I needed more. I lifted up and guided his cock into me, groaning as I felt his hard heat stretch me and fill me.

I gasped in anticipation as I started grinding harder against him, feeling an orgasm building deep inside . . . an orgasm that had been days in the making. We moved together in that throne-like chair in perfect rhythm until I was overcome with the need for release. I let out a soft cry of satisfaction, holding him close, riding him harder. My pussy clenched down on his cock, my slick, tight walls squeezing him until he abruptly pulled out of me.

Before I could ask why he'd done that, Hatter took off his hat, picked me up in his strong arms, and laid me down on the table in front of him. In front of Chess and Callister and Dormouse and everyone else.

My head fell back against a soft, tall half-eaten cake that instantly became a sweet pillow. Then he spread my legs wide apart, knocking over teacups and a vase of roses before driving his hard, wet cock back into my pussy. He planted himself deep into me as he flicked his damp thumb over my swollen clit. Just before I was about to come, he pulled out his cock and shot a deviant grin down at me.

"Why did you stop? I was just about to come again!" I howled in frustration while reaching for his hard shaft. He backed away just beyond my grasp, then grinned even wider.

"You're being a very greedy girl, Alice," he said playfully, waving a finger in reprimand while shaking his head in mock reproach. "What about what *I* want?"

"What do you want?"

I gazed at him expectantly, waiting for his response.

"I want to do something a bit mad," he said, his voice low and gruff. "I want to fuck you *here*."

He grasped his cock and pressed the head against

the tight, pink, wet entrance of my ass. My body was trembling as a drop of precum seeped out of the tip, glistening on his shaft like morning dew.

I shook my head.

"You're insane!"

"I know!" he laughed, and I heard the maniacal tinge that told me I was in for one hell of a ride. The crazed grin was still plastered on his face. "I'm the Mad Hatter, darling. And you have absolutely *no* idea what your gorgeous ass is doing to me."

"Nobody has ever fucked me there," I stammered. My cheeks flushed bright pink with embarrassment as I heard the murmurs and whispers of party guests all around me.

Hatter blinked in surprise, as if my confession was music to his ears. It might've been the sweetest music he'd ever heard.

"Never *ever*?"

"Nope."

"Surely you're joking," he said, caressing my cheeks in his warm hands. "Your ass was made to be fucked. It's beautiful."

As if to prove his point, he spread my ass cheeks apart and massaged the tight entrance until I groaned in desire.

"Let me be the first."

"I don't know," I hesitated. "Is it going to hurt?"

"I promise you'll love it," Hatter crooned. He dipped a finger into my pussy and then slid the wet digit into my dark passage, feeling it tighten around him. "How do you like this?"

"It feels good," I admitted.

"What about this?" he asked, slipping in a second finger. He played with my hole until I got used to the sensation. "Do you still like it?"

"It's kind of a lot," I admitted.

"What if I do this?" Without waiting for a response, Hatter bowed his head and sealed his mouth over the delicate folds of my pussy, licking with broad strokes before sucking gently on my swollen clit.

I bucked against his face, and he rewarded my movements by thrusting his fingers deeper into my ass, wriggling and fluttering them until I whimpered. He brought me right to the edge of orgasm, then stood up and gazed down at me.

"Did you enjoy that?"

"Yeah," I moaned as he continued pumping his fingers in and out of me. "Oh Hatter . . . don't stop."

"Does that mean you enjoy taking in the ass?"

I'd never felt anything like it before, and I wasn't expecting it to feel so good.

I nodded my head.

“Say it out loud.”

“I like it.”

“What do you like?”

“I like your fingers in my ass.”

Hatter's bright blue eye gleamed with anticipation, while his brown one blazed with mischief.

"Good girl," he said softly. "Why, you're such a good girl that I'm going to give you something even better now. I think you're ready."

Suddenly the fingers disappeared. Before I could register what was happening, I felt Hatter's warm hands on my waist as he flipped me over and shoved my face-first onto the table. He grabbed my wrists and pinned them beside my head.

"Take it for me, Alice," he commanded. "I know you can handle it."

With a wail of humiliating pleasure and pain, the crown of Hatter's hot, hard cock pressed into my entrance, burning as he stretched me wider than I'd ever imagined possible. Clutching onto the tablecloth beneath my fingers, I gasped as he slowly worked his length inside my tight hole. One delicious inch at a time, he conquered my untouched depths until he was embedded down to the hilt of his shaft.

I struggled as the sensations raced through my veins, each wave of pleasure more intense than the last. I was torn between wanting to push him away, to reject the experience of being ravaged by this man in such a way. But every cell in my body savored the forbidden pleasure that only increased with every thrust from Hatter.

A low, guttural groan of surrender fought its way out of my chest as I got acclimated to the strange, unfamiliar sensation. His movements were gentle and controlled, allowing me to adjust to his size.

As he started to fuck me, I heard him moan against my ear.

"What about now? How does it feel to have my cock this deep in your untouched, virgin ass? Do you still like it?"

I trembled with desire, both scared and aroused by this man's power over my body. Even though it shamed me to be taken like this in front of so many people, part of me reveled in being used in such a depraved way. I swallowed hard and tried to push down the rebellious thoughts running through my mind. Part of me wanted to scream how humiliating it was to have this man's cock skewering me in such a degrading way.

But the truth was that it only excited me more to be his little fuck toy.

"Yeah," I whimpered while nodding my head. "It still feels good."

Hatter laughed under his breath.

"I knew it would. What does it feel like? Be a good girl and tell everyone here *exactly* what you're feeling."

I let out a shudder as Hatter adjusted his hips, taking care not to ride me too hard. A new wave of pleasure surged through me.

"It's a strange sensation. I feel so full . . . like I'm going to explode. It's like I'm being filled up in a way I've never imagined before," I confessed, unable to properly describe the emotions that left me both elated and scared. "It's intense and kind of overwhelming . . . but it feels amazing."

"Do you want me to fuck you harder?"

"Yeah," I whimpered.

"Then say it, Alice," he urged. "Be a good little slut and tell me exactly what you want me to do to you."

"I want you to fuck me," I whispered, afraid to admit just how much I wanted him.

"Where do you want me to fuck you?"

"In my ass."

Hatter let out a wicked laugh and increased the slow thrusts of his hips. I gasped as he moved faster, his thick heat radiating through my body with each little movement he made.

"Say it louder for me," he said.

“Fuck my in my ass,” I whispered.

“Louder.”

"I want you to fuck me in my ass!" I yelled.

His eyes lit up in delight as he gripped my hips and slammed deep into me. He glided in and out of me at a steady pace, building up the intensity until my breath was coming in short gasps, each stroke more powerful than the previous one. I felt his hips grinding against my ass, pushing me further and further into the tablecloth. The dishes and silverware spread out on the table rattled with every one of Hatter's thrusts, each one of them sending a shudder through my body.

"It's too much," I groaned. "I can't take any more."

But Hatter didn't stop. He let go of my wrists and pushed further and further, until I thought I'd break apart. The moment he slipped his fingers into my pussy and began to massage my clit, I arched my back and pushed against him, aching to be filled and desperate for more.

Hatter was unlike any lover I had ever known. His touch was electric, sending jolts of pleasure coursing through my veins, while his whispers were laced with madness, enticing me further into the depths of my own lust.

In the throes of passion, I felt as if I was teetering on the edge of sanity, my mind and heart racing with equal intensity. And as Hatter pushed me past my limits, I discovered a newfound power within myself, an unyielding determination that would see me through the darkest corners of Wonderland's twisted reality.

He battered away at my tightness, constructing new realms of pleasure from my innocence. My stomach tensed up and I was lost in the moment, my body completely possessed by the sensations rising within me before spiraling out of control. I caught Callister's gaze, torn between disgust and utter fascination by my actions. His tongue slowly slid out of his mouth and wetted his bottom lip before he bit down on it with restrained hunger.

I thought about what it would feel like to have him fucking me at the same time. Maybe he'd fuck my mouth while Chess and Hatter filled my pussy and my ass. Maybe he'd pinch my nipples or play with my clit while his friends took turns fucking me.

Another orgasm tore through my core, ripping through my body and making me cry out so loud that the birds in the trees shot into the air and flew away.

"Oh, Alice . . . " Hatter groaned as my slick walls convulsed around his fingers and my dark orifice tightened around his cock. He sped up his thrusts and pounded into me even harder, making me scream in pleasure. "Fuck, Alice, you feel incredible! You have no idea what you're doing to me!"

With his fingers still anchored in my pussy, I felt him thrust into my ass as deep as he could before his breath caught in his throat. He hissed in ecstasy as all of his hot cum spilled into the soft heat of my channel.

Tea cups rattled on their saucers with every final slam as Hatter emptied his balls into me, one warm spurt after another. Finally he fell backwards into his overstuffed chair, pulling me down with him, his cock lodged inside my ass until it stopped twitching.

I lay against his heaving chest in a delirious daze, my dress stuck to me with sweat, trembling with satisfaction while Hatter and I caught our breath. He held me close, stroking my frosting-coated blonde hair absentmindedly. Then he kissed my shoulder, his lips lingering for a moment before he pulled away.

"That was incredible," he whispered. "Did you enjoy that?"

Too overwhelmed with pleasure to speak right away, I could only nod.

"Good," Hatter said with a relaxed sigh and a wide grin. "I'm so proud of you for being able to take my cock. I can't wait to do it again."

I didn't even mind the guests who were watching me recover from the thorough fucking I'd just received.

I knew that I should feel ashamed for what had just transpired, but instead, a newfound power surged through my veins, leaving me feeling invincible.

"You sound pretty relaxed," I whispered softly, my fingers trailing a delicate path along Mad Hatter's neck. "Are you going to tell me where you hid the Vorpal Sword?"

A gentle laugh tumbled out of Hatter's chest, his eyes glinting with contentment in the dimly lit garden.

"I suppose you've earned your prize, haven't you?" He shifted me until his cock slipped out of my ass, then zipped up his pants before pulling me back into his lap. He leaned against the arm of his chair, propping himself up on an elbow as he gazed at me in what I hoped was approval. "Very well, then."

He traced his fingertips along my collarbone, drawing idle patterns as he spoke. "The sword lies hidden within the heart of a treacherous labyrinth, guarded by a deadly chessboard that has claimed the lives of many who dared to venture there."

He lifted a brow and grinned at me.

"But I doubt those poor souls studied fencing for six years. I'm sure you'll do fine. Especially if I go with you. I'll take you to the entrance of the maze when you're ready."

"The more, the merrier," murmured Chess, who hadn't left his chair since we'd arrived. "I'm impressed by this new, fiery version of Alice," he said, leaning closer to where I still sat curled up in Hatter's lap. "Besides, my shape-shifting abilities could prove useful in navigating the dangers that await you. What about you, Callister? Will you join us?"

The corner of Callister's mouth twitched, but he shook his head.

"I don't think so. I have business to attend to."

"What sort of business?"

Callister crossed his arms over his chest and tilted his head to one side, carefully considering his answer.

"I have business with the King of Clubs. Need I say more?"

Chess shook his head in a way that suggested the King of Clubs was all the explanation necessary.

Nobody had mentioned him before, but he must've been someone important.

How could he not be?

He was a fucking *king*.

"When should we leave to go find the sword?" I asked Chess and Hatter.

"First thing in the morning," Hatter said, giving my ass a playful smack before finding his hat and slapping it back onto his head. "You're welcome to spend the night with me, but you won't get much sleep if you do. Chess knows where the spare bedrooms are. Take your pick. We can celebrate more after your imminent victory."

I took a deep breath, inhaling the thick, musty air that seemed to cling to every corner of the Mad Hatter's property. My heart pounded in my chest, fueled by a newfound sense of confidence and determination.

I was no longer just a party girl from LA seeking

an escape from my life being lived under a microscope. Here, in Wonderland, nobody seemed to judge me at all. I was a fighter—a warrior. I'd kicked Callister's ass in our duel of imaginations. I felt ready to face the obstacles that lay ahead.

And if I could find my way through a Costco on a Saturday, I could sure as hell get through a maze. With a Cheshire Cat demon and a Mad Hatter by my side, there was no challenge too great for me to conquer.

"You really think I have what it takes?"

Hatter gave a soft laugh and winked at Chess.

"I know you do, Alice. I know you do."

CHAPTER EIGHT

CHESS

I kept a protective eye on Alice as she, Hatter, and I traversed the bizarre landscape of Wonderland. Thanks to the Red Queen's madness wandering past the point of no return, our surroundings had become a twisted mockery of the world we'd always known.

I'd gotten used to the perpetual rot and decay that infected the land like a disease. But even demons like me enjoy sunshine and rainbows every now and then.

Yet I couldn't remember the last time I'd seen sunbeams kissing a garden in full bloom, and I'd forgotten how much I longed to see such things.

Until I met Alice.

She was an explosion of color in our miserable grey world, bringing everything around her back to life . . . whether she knew it or not. And I wanted more.

So much more.

I watched her shapely legs step among the gnarled

and misshapen tree roots while branches reached out like the arms of tormented souls. Shadows seemed to dance around us and contort unnaturally. I was of the ether—I was used to such things. But it was the creatures of this forest that truly defied logic: they were grotesque amalgamations of nightmares and animals, created with a few too many eyes or not enough limbs. They slithered or skulked just beyond our path.

"Chess, what exactly are those?" Alice inquired, her voice a mixture of curiosity and unease as she pointed towards a pair of monstrous beasts. They were part reptile and part arachnid, their scales glistening beneath a glistening layer of viscous, venomous slime.

"Ah, those would be skitter-scales," I replied with a wry grin, though I could tell she wasn't amused. "Best not to touch them, my dear. Their bite is . . . unpleasant."

"Everything in this forest seems unpleasant, if you ask me," Hatter chimed in, his wild mismatched eyes darting from one distorted shadow to another. I could tell that his madness was starting to creep back into his brain, but I kept quiet about it. Sometimes bringing attention to something, even the absence of something, only made it more powerful.

I needed Hatter in top form to help us find the Vorpal Sword.

So far, we hadn't even found the entrance to the maze.

As we continued on, an uncomfortable sensation

settled over us like a heavy fog. It was undeniable–we were being watched, and likely followed. I cast a sidelong glance at Hatter, and he met my gaze with a knowing look.

"You feel it too, don't you?" Hatter asked me, his voice low and cautious.

"Feel what?" asked Alice. My loins stirred at her innocent question. Despite her depraved antics from the previous night, she still had much to learn.

So much.

I looked forward to teaching her, once we were somewhere safe and out of danger.

"The prickling at the back of your neck–" Hatter explained as he shivered dramatically. "Do you feel the sense that we're being stalked by an unseen predator?"

"I definitely feel it . . . without question," I confirmed quietly, my demon senses heightened.

"Maybe it's Callister?" Alice suggested. I immediately shook my head.

"He's cunning and occasionally manipulative, but he's not overtly malicious. Whatever is following us, they have death on their minds."

Alice's eyes opened wide.

"How can you tell?"

"Thoughts belong to the ether," I said, trying to explain as best as I could. "I belong to the ether. I exist on the same frequency, so I feel it. That's how I knew that you wanted to ride me like a hobby horse. I felt your thoughts."

Hatter laughed softly, his eyes flickering over to Alice.

"You want to ride Chess like a hobby horse? Let me guess—he made you come, but he wouldn't fuck you, would he?"

A hot flush of pink spread across Alice's face, giving Hatter his answer without her having to say a word.

"I let her ride my face, but it wasn't enough for our insatiable little libertine," I told him with an air of playful indignation. "I promised to fuck her properly once she's out of danger."

"I'm glad you made her wait," said Hatter as he ran his hand down the curve of Alice's back before squeezing her ass through her dress. My inner demon growled with hunger as I watched her body respond to him.

Pert breasts rose higher as her back arched against his hand. I could smell the nectar pooling in her cunt. My mouth began to water, and I felt my cock stir. It was mild torture for this Cheshire Cat not to taste the cream.

My pupils widened as I watched Hatter lean down close to Alice's ear.

"All that pussy licking and tongue fucking Chess did certainly worked in my favor. Not that I would've minded the challenge of trying harder to seduce you, Alice."

Alice pressed her dark pink lips together in mock frustration, and she tossed her long blonde hair over her shoulder. It was obvious she was trying to act nonchalant, yet I could practically feel how badly her cunt ached to be filled . . . to be stretched.

As soon as we found that damned sword, I would stuff her to the brim.

"Maybe I won't fuck you again," she teased Hatter, which made me grin wide. "Or maybe you'll have to work harder to get with this." She lifted the back of her skirt high enough to flash us both her firm, tan, bare ass cheek, and I saw Hatter clench his jaw. I knew what he was thinking, because again, his thoughts belonged to the ether, the same as me.

He wanted to shove Alice to the ground, push up her dress, and fuck her from behind.

Hard.

I'd politely stand back and watch him pump a load into her, and then I'd have a turn. I'd skewer that tight, greedy cunt with my demon cock and make her forget that Hatter had been there right before me.

I'd make her forget her fucking *name*.

Suddenly I heard a twig snap. The sound was nearly inaudible, but loud enough for me to hear. I held up my hand to get Alice and Hatter's attention, then pressed my finger to my lips.

I closed my eyes to focus in the silence of the forest. My demon senses reached out through the twisted landscape like tendrils of a vine, probing the shadows for any sign of hidden foes. I felt the presence of four beings lurking nearby, their malevolent intent clear as day.

"Four soldiers loyal to the Red Queen are hiding in our midst," I whispered to Alice and Hatter, my eyes still closed as I held onto the connection. "And they're gaining on us."

"Why would anyone be following us in the first place?" Alice asked, her dark blonde brows furrowing in concern. "What do they want?"

"*You*, most likely," Hatter told her, his voice ominous. "Someone must've told the Red Queen that you're here. If it was the shy Violet, I'll kill her myself!"

"I'd bet my soul that it was Dinah," I whispered, opening my eyes to take a cautious look around.

"Don't be absurd, Chess," Hatter hissed. "You're a demon! You have no soul!"

Ignoring him, I shook my head.

"Dinah's been pretending to be Alice's friend for years," I explained. "She's been feeding her blue pills to make her forget her connection to Wonderland."

Hatter cast me a skeptical glance.

"Blue pills? Are you sure about that?"

Alice stopped walking and turned around to face Hatter and me.

"Dude, I barfed one up right after I got here, and it turned into a giant worm and started crawling!"

"Callister stepped on it, but it's possible that someone found its residue," I told them. "The Red Queen's soldiers must've found it during their patrols."

Hatter's blue eye lit up in dark amusement while his brown eye glinted dangerously. He cracked the knuckles in each of his fists, flexing his hands in preparation for a right.

"Well, let's see if we can persuade them to come out and play, shall we?"

As if on cue, four of the Red Queen's soldiers emerged from the shadows. They were clad in menacing armor, black as night, with red rose symbols adorning their chests. Their deadly weapons were drawn, ready to strike at a moment's notice.

"Ah, there you are!" Hatter called out mockingly, clapping his hands together in feigned delight. "We've been expecting you!"

"Silence!" one of the soldiers barked, stepping forward. "Alice, you are hereby ordered by Her Majesty the Red Queen to come with us immediately!"

"Oh yeah?" Alice retorted, folding her arms and glaring defiantly at the soldier. "Well, tell her she can go shove it."

"Such insolence," another soldier sneered, tightening his grip on his weapon. "You'll pay dearly for that."

"Really, gentlemen, there's no need for such hostility," I chimed in, my grin widening as I felt the power coursing through me, preparing for what was to come.

On the surface, all the soldiers could see was a dark-haired man wearing a purple and black tiger-striped suit. But underneath the clothes and the skin, my blood was simmering with charged-up magic. Once it exploded, there was no reining it back in.

"I'm sure we can all come to some sort of agreement."

"The Red Queen does not negotiate!" the first soldier shouted back at me. "We will take Alice by force, if necessary!"

"Good luck with that," Hatter snickered, his madness shining through even in the face of danger. When two of the soldiers pulled out their swords, Alice's eyes widened at the seriousness of the situation.

"What can I do to help?" she asked, her voice dropping with worry. Keeping his eyes pinned on the soldiers, Hatter tilted his head in her direction.

"Get behind Chess and try to conjure a weapon to protect yourself with. It's about to get messy."

Alice blinked in hopeless confusion. It was one thing to challenge Callister in the relative safety of Hatter's back garden. It was another thing altogether for her to arm herself and prepare to defend her own life.

I locked eyes with Hatter, and we exchanged a determined glance. Alice was our responsibility now.

She was our lover, our heroine, our everything—and we would protect her at all costs from the Red Queen.

"I'll always be ready to protect you," Hatter replied, his tone playful yet I knew he was deadly serious.

"As will I," I murmured, feeling my demon powers surge through me as I prepared for battle. Pivoting to the four soldiers, I gave them a short, ceremonial bow.

"Very well, gentlemen. Let's dance."

The soldiers charged at us, their weapons glinting in the dappled light. My body began to contort and shift, muscles rippling and bones cracking as I transformed into a massive, fearsome beast.

My limbs throbbed and my skin ripped open, the seams of my existence violently ripping apart, a saturation of muscles, sinews, and blood vessels snaking under my skin, rendering me a hideous monster. I towered over them, the air thick with menace and bloodlust. My mouth stretched wide, revealing rows of razor-sharp teeth that gleamed hungrily, desperate to taste their flesh.

"What madness is this?" one soldier cried out, stumbling backward in terror.

But he didn't get very far.

I lunged forward, my claws sinking deep into his armor, tearing through metal and flesh like they were one and the same. Blood sprayed across my face, hot and metallic, as the man fell lifeless to the ground. An artery continued to spurt out a thin arc of blood, painting the twisted trees a dark crimson.

"Get away!" another soldier screamed, swinging his sword at my monstrous form. His weak attempts were laughable—I swatted him aside with a single swipe of my enormous paw.

The force of the blow sent him crashing into the distorted shadows of the surreal landscape. His body hit the ground with a hard thud, until he lay still, his limbs and neck contorted in the most unnatural of ways.

"Chess, you magnificent beast!" Hatter cackled,

his madness fueling his courage as he threw himself into the fray. Keeping Alice safe between us, he leapt forward and started slashing at the nearest soldier.

His movements were erratic and unpredictable, making it impossible for his opponent to anticipate his next strike. With each powerful swing of the blade, the scent of fresh blood filled the air, accompanied by cries of pain and terror.

“It’s almost too easy," Hatter mused, slicing through another soldier's armor as if it were paper. "You lot really should've brought more friends."

Just at that moment, I realized what Alice was holding in her hands.

“A cast-iron frying pan?” I teased. “Is that your idea of conjuring a weapon?”

“I panicked!” she gasped with a shrug.

My heart swelled with pride and admiration for her. Here she was, tapping into reserves of strength and cunning that Hatter and I didn't know she possessed.

A frying pan wasn’t my first choice of weapon, but it had its uses.

Alice stood en garde, and our movements became fluid and synchronized, like the intricate choreography of a deadly ballet. We had become a twisted trinity, bound together by desire and defiance.

“Chess! Watch out!” I heard her yell. I whirled around just in time to see her swing the frying pan against a soldier’s helmet. A clang of metal rang out through the forest as I grabbed his leg in one paw and flung him away.

“Is that all you’ve got?” I roared, my voice a guttural snarl that echoed through the twisted woods. The two remaining soldiers hesitated, their bravado faltering in the face of my ferocity.

"Your psychotic queen won't save you now!" Hatter taunted, his eyes blazing with determination as he brandished his favorite weapon—a flaming sword that burned with flames as blue as his eye. The metal seemed to shimmer with an otherworldly energy, like the sword itself was alive and eager to taste blood.

As I continued tearing through the soldiers, Hatter's laughter echoed in my ears. The madness in his mismatched eyes was equaled only by the wild grin on his face as he danced around our foes. He wove his way in and out of their reach with an unearthly grace that seemed to heighten his insanity.

"Retreat!" one of the soldiers cried out, and the other one began to flee. But I wouldn't let them escape so easily—not after they'd threatened my precious Alice.

I lunged once more, my jaws closing around the third soldier's leg. With a savage twist of my head, I tore it clean off, the sickening crunch of bone filling the night air.

Blood gushed from the stump, pooling around the poor fool as he screamed in agony. His eyes widened with terror as he stared up at me, knowing his fate was sealed.

"Please," he croaked, tears streaming down his cheeks. "Have mercy!”

"Mercy?" I echoed, my voice dripping with disdain. "Like the mercy you would've shown Alice?"

"We wouldn't have harmed her!" the soldier blubbered. "Our instructions were to bring her to Her Majesty alive!"

I lifted an eyebrow.

"Curiouser and curiouser," I mused. "And what are the Red Queen's plans once she has Alice in her possession?"

"I don't know."

I reached one of my paws forward and sank my claws into the bleeding stump where the man's leg used to be. He let out an unholy sound.

"I'm telling you, I don't know!"

"Who told the Red Queen that Alice was here?"

"I don't know her name," the man panted. I growled, then slowly clawed at his flesh like I was casually shuffling a deck of cards. Another wretched scream pushed out of his lungs.

"It began with a D!" he coughed. "Diane or Deena . . . something like that!"

"Was it Dinah, perhaps?"

"Yes!" he cried. "Yes, her name was Dinah! I remember now! She's been assigned to keep track of Alice's whereabouts. That's all I know!"

I frowned at him.

Then I grinned.

"Are you certain about that?" I flexed my paw and shredded the flesh even deeper, until the soldier punched the ground with his fist.

"Chess," Hatter said, laying a hand on my

monstrous shoulder. "You know as well as I do that Alice won't be any safer if this poor bastard suffers or does not."

"Fine," I growled, releasing the soldier from my grip. He crumpled into himself, sobbing in relief, but his reprieve would be short-lived.

He and I both knew that even if he managed to get back onto his horse and return to the Court of Hearts and Roses, the Red Queen would show him no mercy for failing his mission.

The second he turned up without Alice, the queen would be sure to yell, "Off with his head!"

I might be a demon, but I wasn't a monster. It would be a kindness to take care of it here, and end his suffering sooner.

I growled, then shifted my monstrous form back into that of a man. I nodded at the hulking fae who stood beside me. A soft whoosh of Hatter's blade made short work of the last remaining soldier.

"Is that the last of them?" Alice asked breathlessly from behind the safety of her frying pan. Her blue eyes were busy scanning the forest for any remaining threats. She might not have had our supernatural abilities or experience, but she had proven herself to be incredibly resourceful—and determined to prove herself.

"Seems so," said Hatter as he stole a few coins off each of the bodies.

"Nice teamwork, guys," Alice smirked, wiping a stray droplet of gore from her cheek.

"You were pretty impressive yourself," I replied,

feeling the weight of our actions settle heavily upon my shoulders.

It wasn't that I felt bad about killing the Red Queen's soldiers. I was simply concerned that their deaths would only make the Red Queen more desperate for Alice's head.

Her beautiful, sassy, kissable head.

I couldn't let that happen.

Not to her.

My gaze swiveled down to the ground, taking in the sight of one soldier's exposed flesh from his abdomen. His entrails had spilled out onto the ground in a steaming mass of gore and viscera.

The smell of blood and sweat filled the air, mingling with the eerie whispers of the twisted trees. I closed my eyes and sent a silent message to the fauna of the forest to come to our aid.

"We can't linger here," I said when I was done. "The Red Queen will surely send more soldiers after us."

"Chess is right," Hatter agreed, his eyes clouded with concern. "We need to move, and quickly."

"Where do we go?" Alice questioned, her voice shaking slightly as the adrenaline began to wear off. Her eyes were wide, taking in the altered landscape around us, a world warped and wild, its strange creatures watching from behind gnarled trees and grotesque stones.

Damn, she was stunning. Especially when covered in the blood of our enemies. I felt a sudden urge to pull her against my body and press my cock against her warm gash before spreading her wide open for my inhuman flesh . . . but now was not the time.

“We’ll find somewhere safe," I answered, knowing full well that safety was a rare commodity in this twisted Wonderland. “We need to get as far away from the Red Queen's reach as possible."

"*Is* there such a place?" Hatter mused, his gaze sweeping across the horizon, searching for any sign of sanctuary. “Not even the White Queen’s castle will be safe for long.”

"We need to regroup and plan our next move."

"Then let's not waste any more time," Alice said, determination blazing in her eyes.

"Lead the way, Chess,” Hatter urged, sheathing his bloodstained blade.

We’d only taken a few steps when flashes of light pink appeared in every direction and zipped right past us.

“Oh shit!” Alice groaned with a grimace. “Guys, do you see the fuzzy pink bunnies?”

I yawned and nodded my head. The battle had taken more out of me than I realized.

“Yes. I sent for them.”

Alice stopped in her tracks, but Hatter grasped her by the waist and turned to watch the spectacle that was unfolding before us.

“You can watch them with me, if you want to,” he said, shooting a wild-eyed look of amusement at Alice. “They’re not here for us.”

Sure enough, the pink bunnies were swarming

the bodies of the dead soldiers. Within a matter of minutes, the flesh was stripped off the bone, and then the bones were gnawed away into oblivion. Gruesome as it was, it was too fascinating for any of us to look away.

The only thing that remained of the queens' men was their armor. While the fuzzy pink bunnies groomed their blood-stained fur, the vines and plants of the forest quickly grew over the soldiers' armor and hid all traces of their existence from view.

"We should probably go now that the bunnies are fed and full," I said to Alice and Hatter. After walking in a small circle, trying to gauge which way we'd come from when the soldiers had found us, I looked at my old friend. "Hatter? Are we still headed in the right direction?"

Hatter turned his wild, mismatched eyes to me, and I found myself faltering at the madness that bloomed within them. His mouth spread into a wide grin, and felt my Cheshire smile fading away.

I didn't want to say it out loud, but I was . . . concerned.

Our guide was starting to lose his grasp on reality.

I couldn't let Alice know.

Not now.

Not when she was riding so high on such a wave of confidence.

No, it was my job to keep her morale up, and to keep Hatter focused. He was the only one who knew where the Vorpal Sword was hidden.

"If we're not here, then we're there . . . but

soldiers might be anywhere," sang Hatter, his wild eyes darting about. "But as long as we stay ahead of the Red Queen's minions, it matters little where we find ourselves."

"All valid points. Remember to keep your guard up," I said, my own senses on high alert. "We've already killed four of the Red Queen's soldiers. As soon as she realizes they're missing, she'll be coming for us with all she has."

As we began our hasty retreat from the site of the battle, I couldn't help but marvel at the bond that had formed between us. Three unlikely allies, brought together by fate and bound by a common goal: to bring down the Red Queen and restore balance to Wonderland.

And as the sinister landscape stretched out before us, I knew that together, we just might have a fighting chance.

CHAPTER NINE

ALICE

The air hung heavy with the scent of decay as Chess, Hatter and I trudged through the twisted landscape of Wonderland. The ground beneath our feet was slick with slime and rot, making each step a precarious endeavor.

I slipped more than a couple of times and was luckily caught by my two companions. Hatter and Chess walked alongside me, protective as ever, their eyes watchful in the dark and the gloom.

"Hey, guys . . . I'm curious," I said, my voice laced with frustration, "why has Callister been so completely unhelpful when I've gone out of my way to prove what I'm capable of? Doesn't he want to save Wonderland?"

"Callister has his reasons," Hatter replied, his voice distant, as if he were lost in thought. "He's not one to trust easily."

"Maybe he's just an asshole," I said under my

breath, recalling the countless snide remarks Callister had thrown my way since we'd met.

"You're not wrong about that," Chess agreed, his green eyes glittering mysteriously in the murky light. "But it's not without reason. He's seen what the Red Queen can do firsthand."

"What do you mean?"

"The Red King was Callister's brother, and their loyalty to each other ran deep," Chess began, his voice somber as we continued our trek through the decaying forest.

"It still runs deep, even in death," Hatter added. "When The Red Queen ordered the king to lose his head, it nearly destroyed Callister and the rest of Wonderland."

"The king was the only person who could temper the Red Queen's irrational fits of rage," Chess explained.

"That's awful," I replied, feeling a deep ache in my heart.

I finally understood that Callister wasn't an asshole . . . he was grieving, and I wanted to do something to comfort him. I wished there was something I could do, some way to bring his brother back or undo the damage inflicted by the Red Queen.

But all I could do was find the Vorpal Sword and kill something called a Jabberwocky.

It sounded so outlandish, but I was dreaming. And even if I wasn't, it was still a lot to process. I needed to take things one step at a time.

"What did Callister's brother do that made the Red Queen so angry?" I asked after a little more walking. "Was he cheating on her? Was he planning to steal her throne?"

Chess and Hatter shared a weary glance before Hatter shook his head.

"You're not remotely close," said Chess. "The Red Queen's rage boiled over when she discovered the Red King had placed a bright pink flower on her bedside table. Everyone in the Kingdom of Hearts and Roses knows that the Red Queen must *only* have red roses. Not pink, not purple, and for heaven's sake, *never* white. They must only be red. She took this to mean the king no longer loved her and she had him beheaded that same day."

"She put his head on a spike in the center of her rose garden as a reminder to everyone in her court," Hatter chimed in.

"What the actual *fuck*?" I gasped. "How is she still in power?"

"Simple," Chess shrugged. "Everyone's terrified of her."

"That's why you have to defeat her," said Hatter. "I think Callister might be jealous that it has to be you," he added with a bitter laugh. "He'd rather it was him. Can you imagine losing your brother because his delusional wife was angry over the color of a *flower*? No wonder Callister is the way he is."

I felt a dark, ugly wave of disgust run through me at the thought. The Red Queen was truly monstrous, even by Wonderland's twisted standards. "What else has she done?" I asked, eager for more ammunition against my enemy.

"What else has she done? Oh, Alice . . . Alice . . . where do we even begin?" Hatter pondered, his eyes gleaming with a manic light as he recounted the atrocities committed by the deranged ruler. "She ordered the beheading of every rose gardener who planted pink or white roses instead of red. An honest mistake, but the woman couldn't abide anything that wasn't a direct order from her."

"Then there was the time she transformed an entire village into stone statues," Chess interjected, the horror of the memory flickering across his handsome features. "All because they failed to pay tribute to her on her birthday. She didn't care that they were starving, or that their crops were destroyed by her own hand."

"She ordered fireworks to be set off in the middle of a drought because she was bored one evening," Hatter said.

"The crops went up in flames, all while she watched from her balcony," said Chess. "And she ordered the fire brigade to stay near the castle so it wouldn't burn down. Half the village was left homeless, and all of them were starving, so she simply turned them to stone. Problem solved."

As we navigated the treacherous terrain, Hatter and Chess regaled me with tales of the Red Queen's insane rage and murderous ways. They talked about how she had forced her own subjects to dance upon hot coals for her entertainment, their screams echoing through the night like a twisted symphony.

I could only stare in stunned silence.

The woman was crazier than the Mad Hatter and the March Hare combined.

"She's absolutely batshit crazy, isn't she?" I asked.

"Her insanity knows no bounds." Hatter shook his head, a mixture of anger and sorrow etched upon his face. "She even tried to force a marriage between herself and the King of Spades, just to consolidate power. Thankfully, it never came to pass. The King of Spades declared himself to be so deep in debt that the Queen decided it was more hassle to marry him than it was worth."

"But if the King of Spades married her, wouldn't he be able to take over the Red Queen's throne?"

Hatter burst into shrieks of laughter while Chess merely shook his head.

"Not likely," said Chess. "Wonderland is similar to the game of chess in that Queens are always more powerful than Kings."

"Even if the kings are young and strong," Hatter added. "Makes no difference. Queens will always outrank a king."

"Wow! She's worse than I imagined!" I whispered, my fists clenched in righteous fury. Not only had she terrorized Wonderland's people with her brutality, but she'd torn families apart, leaving scars that would never fully heal.

She'd hurt Callister.

"Yes, she's worse than *anyone* could've ever imagined," Chess agreed, placing a reassuring hand on my shoulder. "But you mustn't let your anger consume you. It's exactly what she wants—for us all to become as twisted and broken as she is."

The more I heard, the angrier I became—not just at the Red Queen, but also at Callister for his lack of support in helping me save Wonderland.

"She wants us twisted and broken . . . just like Callister?" I suggested offhandedly.

"He's nothing like her," Chess replied with a slight bite to his words, making me wonder if I'd hit a nerve.

Still, I pushed again.

"If Callister has so much to gain by getting rid of the queen, then why would he stand by and let me struggle? He should be here with us, but instead he's just puffing his life away."

Sensing my frustration, Chess put a tender hand on my shoulder.

"Perhaps Callister has given up hope that anyone can truly change things here. But you, Alice, are different. You have shown us all that there is still hope, and that is something worth fighting for. That's why I'm helping you."

"Same here," Hatter said with a twisted, loopy grin.

"Still," I insisted, "I've busted my ass to get this far. I just want Callister to believe in me."

"You don't need him to believe in you," Hatter

said to me, suddenly serious, "You're stronger than you give yourself credit for. Don't give up, Alice."

"I won't," I vowed, my resolve hardening as I clutched Hatter's hand tighter. "No matter what it takes, I'll do whatever I can to get rid of the Red Queen and make your world whole again."

"This is precisely what makes you so captivating," Hatter nodded, his gaze meeting mine with surprising intensity. "We'll go to great lengths to help you take her down, Alice. But whatever we do, we mustn't sink to her level. We're better than that."

"Of course," I agreed, swallowing the bile that was starting to rise in my throat. "I won't become like her. I promise."

"Good. Now, enough talk of the Red Queen and Callister and everything else," Chess murmured, green eyes glowing with approval. "We've arrived."

I'd been so distracted by the horror stories about the Red Queen and being pissy about Callister, only to find out the reason for his pain that I hadn't paid much attention to where we were going.

I looked up, my eyes widening in awe at the sight before us.

A giant wall of dark green leaves shot up out of the ground at least thirty feet into the sky. I ran my fingers along the towering hedge walls as my boots crunched on the gravel path.

Thorny vines twisted in impossible patterns, their shadowy forms flickering across my skin. My heart pounded with equal parts fear and excitement as Hatter felt around the vines in search of the entrance.

"Not here," he hummed, elbow deep in the hedge. Frowning in thought, he took off his top hat, scratched his head, and slapped it back on.

"Maybe over here?" he muttered to himself as he pushed aside vines and felt around some more.

Still nothing.

I glanced at Chess, realizing how far the wall stretched. It was at least the size of SoFi Stadium—maybe even bigger. If Hatter's plan was to feel up a few miles of walls, the three of us were fucked.

And not in the way I was dreaming of.

"Getting closer," Hatter said, pulling out his arm and taking a few more steps.

He carried on with his wall examination for a few more minutes. Just as I was starting to lose my patience, he let out a wild laugh.

"Oh yes . . . I remember now," he snickered, shaking his head. "There is no door."

"No door?" I repeated in disbelief.

"No door," Hatter said with a shrug of his broad shoulders. "We'll have to make one."

"Dude . . . the wall is made of *stone*," I pointed out. "How are we going to get through *stone* if there's no door?"

Hatter was unfazed.

"Imagine it, Alice. Imagine what sort of door this toxic topiary labyrinth would have."

I wrinkled my nose and tried not to glare at him. The guy was a fantastic fuck, but he was also crazy as hell.

"If it's toxic, why would there be a door in the first place?" I asked.

Hatter grinned and shook his head as if I were some kind of idiot to have that thought in the first place.

"Imagine a door," Chess urged as he stepped up by my side. "If the labyrinth inside is made of poisonous plants, what might the entrance to it look like?"

I raised a skeptical brow at them both.

"You're seriously asking me this?"

"Yes."

"Without question."

"Fine," I huffed, folding my arms across my chest. "If it's creepy enough to be made of poisonous plants, then it's probably going to have some kind of gothic, Victorian-style gate."

"What does the gate look like?" Chess asked me. "Be as descriptive as you can."

"Alright, well, it's made of black wrought iron bars and it's really tall and has an arch," I told them, trying to see what was formulating in my mind. "It looks like a gaping mouth, ready to swallow us whole."

"Is it open?" Hatter asked me.

"No, but I can push it open," I told him. "There's no lock. When I push it open, I can see a twisted archway of thorns and withered vines that marks the beginning of the maze."

"Oh, now that is impressive," Hatter murmured. Even Chess hummed in agreement.

"Alice, look what you've done," he said while curling his hand around my waist. He guided me to stand in front of him and Hatter.

I blinked in surprise at what I saw in the wall.

It was the exact gate I'd just imagined in my head and described to the guys.

"Holy shit," I whispered, my heart pounding in my chest. "This place looks worse than my nightmares."

Hatter chuckled darkly, his mismatched eyes gleaming with a wild excitement as he surveyed the sinister garden maze that opened up to us.

"Welcome to Wonderland's underbelly, Alice. Not quite the tea party you were hoping for, is it?"

"Hardly," I replied, my voice trembling despite my best efforts to sound breezy as fuck. My gaze darted about, taking in the grotesque sculptures of rotting flora shaped into monstrous creatures, the ground slick with a viscous slime that reeked of decay. "How are we supposed to find our way through this hellhole?"

"Leave that to me," Hatter said, stepping forward with an air of confidence. "I know these plants better than anyone. Follow my lead, and you'll be safe."

"Safe is a relative term here," Chess said under his breath, his green eyes flickering with unease. He looked at me, his usual sly grin unnervingly absent. "Stay close, Alice. This place is treacherous."

"Trust me, I'm not wandering off anywhere," I assured him. I was going to be glued to his side, whether he liked it or not.

"Good," Hatter said, his gaze locked on the gravel path ahead as he began to lead the way. "Now, pay attention. The first rule of this maze is to never touch anything unless I say otherwise. The plants here are as deadly as they are beautiful."

"Beauty is in the eye of the beholder," I muttered, my eyes narrowing at the writhing vines that seemed to reach for us as we passed.

"Fair enough," Hatter agreed, his voice low and tense. "Take the Bloodthorn Rose, for instance." He pointed to a patch of crimson flowers, their petals glistening with a dark, wet sheen. "One prick from its thorns, and your blood catches fire within your veins. Horrible way to die."

"Charming," I said, shuddering involuntarily as I pointed to a cluster of little white flowers. "What's that plant over there?"

"Ah, the Tears of the Damned," Hatter continued, gesturing to a delicate white flower that wept a viscous black liquid. "The sap from this flower induces a madness so profound, you'll tear yourself apart just to escape it. I've seen someone rip the flesh from their arms after brushing against it. Avoid it at all costs."

"Understood," Chess said, his voice tight with

barely contained fury. "Anything *else* we should know about?"

"Plenty," Hatter replied, his lips curling into a humorless smile. "But fear not; I'll point them out as we go. Just remember—stay close, and listen to me. We'll make it through this nightmare, I promise."

"Here's hoping," I whispered. My mouth had become dry, and my pulse was racing as we ventured further into the toxic labyrinth. With every step we took, I knew our fates were resting on Hatter's unstable wisdom and our own wits.

We delved deeper into the maze, not talking much, which was unlike Hatter. He usually had plenty to say. I took his silence to mean that the horrors that awaited us were far greater than any stupid poisonous plant.

"Chess! We could use your talents right about now!" Hatter abruptly called out, stopping us in our tracks as a cluster of vines gathered in front of us. It looked like a monster made of hundreds of snakes, writhing around as, getting ready to strike.

"Of course," Chess replied, his ethereal form shimmering as his body flattened and took on the shape of a broad shield. I marveled at his transformation, my heart pounding in my chest.

"Stay behind me," he instructed, positioning himself between us and the deadly vines. "I'll clear a path."

"Sounds like a plan," I whispered, clutching Hatter's arm as we followed Chess deeper into the maze.

"Everything all right, Alice?" Hatter asked, his eyes searching mine for any hint of doubt or fear.

"Oh, everything's great. Just great. In fact, it's better than ever," I sarcastically assured him. My pulse was quickening with each step we took, and I was pretty sure if this ball of poisonous snake vines didn't kill us, something else would. "Let's try not to get killed in here, okay?"

"Oh, we can't let you die in here," he said with a low, wicked laugh. "Otherwise you'll never know how it feels to get fucked by a Cheshire Cat demon. Chess has a monster cock, and I want to see you take it for the first time."

Well, that sure as fuck made me forget all about the poisonous snake vines. Still hunched behind Chess as we inched away from the toxic plant, I stole a sideways glance at Hatter. His bright blue eye was twinkling like crazy.

Of course it was.

"You *really* like fucking in front of other people, don't you?" I taunted him.

"I just really like fucking *you*," he said, eyeing my blood-spattered tits. "As soon as we get that Vorpal Sword, I'm going to skewer you with my own. I'm pretty sure Chess won't be content to stand by and watch like he did last time. Tell me, Alice. Have you ever been fucked by two men at once?"

I sucked in a breath of air as my eyes widened. "No."

"Would you like to be?"

"You dirty, dirty man," I scolded, pretending to be offended.

Hatter's grin spread even wider across his handsome face.

"I'll take that as a yes."

"It's definitely not a no," I said as we made our way to safety.

Together Hatter and I watched as Chess shifted back into his human form.

But as he filled out a black and silver leopard print tuxedo, I couldn't help wondering what his monster demon cock looked like.

Would it hurt?

Would it be too big for me? Too long? Too thick?

I licked my lips as I watched him walk in front of me, feeling my core beginning to ache. I wanted him.

I wanted him so bad.

I wanted to seduce him.

To taste him.

To feel him.

To fuck him.

I just needed to live long enough to do it all.

"You will," Chess said, looking over his shoulder at me.

My eyes snapped open in surprise. A seductive grin played on his lips, and I felt a little throb in my clit.

"I'm of the ether, remember? I can hear your thoughts. And I promise you can handle my cock, just as soon as we find the sword."

He reached for my hand, his grip firm yet gentle

as we navigated through the treacherous labyrinth. Part of me wanted to stop right there in the middle of the path and get on all fours, but we had a job to do, and it wasn't a blow job or a hand job.

The poisonous leaves and vines that surrounded us were enough to pull me out of my not-so-private fantasies. Hatter called on Chess to become a bridge over a pool of toxic sludge, and then asked him to morph into a barrier against razor-sharp leaves that threatened to slice us to ribbons.

"Is it just me, or are these plants getting more aggressive?" I asked, watching as a particularly nasty-looking thistle flung itself at Chess's makeshift shield.

"Seems so," Hatter replied, his brow furrowed in concentration. "But we're almost there. Just a little further."

I nodded, my confidence growing with each obstacle we conquered. It was as if Wonderland had awakened something within me, a newfound strength and determination that surged through my veins like liquid fire.

“Is it okay if I take the lead for a while?” I asked, stepping forward with purpose. "I think I see a way through."

"Very well," Hatter conceded, his eyes filled with equal parts admiration and concern. "But be careful."

"Always," I promised, a confident smile on my lips as I navigated the trio through the final section of the maze.

Hatter was so protective. I wondered if he was the kind of guy who'd like it if I called him 'daddy.'

After all, I was pretty good at sitting on his lap while he told me what a good girl I was.

I wondered if he'd still call me a good girl when Chess fed his monster cock into my pussy.

Maybe he'd say it while his dick was in my mouth.

Or my ass.

Fuck! If only!

Suddenly my arm brushed against something that made my skin burn. I looked down to see a nasty looking flower spewing out a cloud of spores.

I gasped and shrieked, getting a lungful of spores that caused searing pain to shoot down my throat. Coughing and choking, I stumbled into another poisonous flower, this time hitting it with my leg. A wave of agony washed over my body.

"Dammit!" I cursed, gritting my teeth as blisters erupted across my skin, each one pulsating with a fiery ache that threatened to drive me insane from the pain.

I wanted to scream, but it hurt too much. If my leg looked this bad, my throat and my lungs were probably the same.

"Oh, Alice! Try not to move," Hatter ordered, his voice laced with barely-contained panic as he carefully lifted me into his strong arms. "If the blisters pop, they'll release more of the spores until we're all covered in them."

My first instinct was to argue with him that it was too dangerous to risk carrying me anywhere, but he couldn't care less.

"Take her over there," Chess instructed, pointing to a place further down the path where a small well had appeared out of nowhere. "We need to wash away the spores before they spread."

Hatter's powerful muscles flexed and moved around me, but all I felt was the painful blisters burning my flesh inside and out. My vision was swimming with tears of pain, and I was so distracted that I didn't realize he'd set me down until I saw him standing above me.

"Hold on, baby. I'll take care of you," Hatter promised, determination etched into his handsome features.

"We both will," said Chess. I loved that he was by my side, although I hated that he wasn't smiling.

Behind him I could see Hatter walking around the maze, his hands deftly plucking leaves and petals from an assortment of nearby plants. I watched him through the haze of pain as he gathered them into a shallow stone bowl that Chess had conjured. He crushed them using a large round stone, releasing fragrant oils that filled the air with an earthy aroma.

The pain in my lungs flared up like fire, then started to fade away as I breathed in the scented oils.

"Chess, hold her still," he said, lifting up a handful of the resulting paste. "This should help, but it's going to feel worse before it feels better."

I felt Chess's strong hands grasp my wrists, holding me down as Hatter spread the paste on my ravaged arm.

I whimpered as it stung like nettles before it

finally began to soothe the pain. Then Chess held down my ankles while Hatter spread more of the paste along the length of my calf and my thigh.

As the blisters began to fade, I felt eternally grateful for my companions, my fucked-up knights in leopard print armor who'd come to my rescue.

I'd given them my body . . .

Now it was time to give them my soul.

My heart ached as I realized the lengths they were willing to go to fight for me when nobody in my life back home would've done anything close.

Reaching my arms up towards my wicked boys of Wonderland, I cupped Hatter's jaw in one hand while caressing Chess's tousled dark hair with the other.

I'd fallen through the rabbit hole, only to realize I was falling for them both.

"Thank you," I whispered, meeting Hatter's wild eyes for the first time since the danger had passed. "I owe you my life."

"You owe me nothing," he replied, a hint of a smile playing on his lips as he helped me sit up.

"Alright, well, I've got your back."

Hatter snickered softly.

Seductively.

Hungrily.

"Is that so? I'd rather have you on *yours*."

My stomach coiled and my core ached with need for him, for Chess, for both of them filling me at once, but not when I was covered in botanical paste and blood from the Red Queen's soldiers.

"I know that's what you'd like," Chess murmured, his velvety voice cutting through my thoughts. "Channel that desire, Alice. Use that energy, that fire to make it through the rest of the maze, and claim the Vorpal Sword. I assure you," he said, his breath warm on my ear as he and Hatter both pulled me to my feet, "the weapon isn't the only prize you'll claim when all's said and done."

CHAPTER TEN

ALICE

We finally reached the end of the maze, and I scrunched my forehead as a peculiar sight unfolded before Hatter, Chess, and me.

The walls of hedges parted to reveal a giant chessboard stretched out in all directions. Its black and red squares gleamed like polished onyx and marble. The pieces were human-sized, grotesque, twisted versions of familiar chess piece shapes.

But the creepiest thing of all was that they were alive.

Their stone eyes were cold and calculating as they plotted their next moves. Suddenly one of the red pieces advanced. Within seconds, a black piece shaped like a horse lunged forward with a jousting spear and attacked.

The piece exploded in a spray of red. All that was left was a pile of red gravel and a cloud of red dust. From where I was standing, it looked a lot like blood.

"Curiouser and curiouser," Chess murmured as my gaze darted from one piece to another. I looked up to find him stroking his chin in thought.

Even Hatter seemed confused, and this entire thing was his creation.

"If they can do that to each other, how the hell are *we* supposed to get across?" I hissed at him.

"Well now, that is the question, isn't it?" Hatter replied, his black eye gleaming with danger while his blue eye sparkled with amusement. "The board is both a puzzle and a death trap. One wrong move, and you'll be at the mercy of these fearsome creatures."

Not wanting to end up as a pile of meat chunks and pink mist, I turned on my heel and folded my botanical salve-caked arms across my chest. The blisters had mostly disappeared, and the salve was dry and starting to crack on my skin.

"*I'll* be at their mercy? What about you guys? You're coming with me, right?"

Hatter cast me an apologetic look from underneath the brim of his top hat and shook his head.

"We can offer guidance and support, but we can't cross the chessboard on your behalf. That is a task you must complete on your own."

"Great," I muttered sarcastically, feeling an all-too-familiar flutter of anxiety in the pit of my stomach.

But it was quickly stifled by the connection I'd forged with Chess, who slinked over to my side. He took me into his arms, gazing at me with his mesmerizing green eyes.

"Don't be afraid, Alice," he said, his voice brimming with confidence. "Together, we can navigate this treacherous game and reach the other side unscathed. Tell me . . . " he murmured as he leaned in close, his breath hot against my ear. "Do you know how to play chess?"

I stiffened, my heart pounding in my chest like a trapped animal. The truth was, I didn't have the faintest idea. My grandpa had tried to teach me when I was younger, but I'd always gotten bored and wandered off before he could finish explaining the rules.

"I don't have a fucking clue," I admitted, hating the way my voice trembled.

"Very well," Chess said, his Cheshire grin spreading across his face. "Pay close attention, and I'll guide you through the game."

"Are you sure you can't just do it for me?" I asked, desperation coloring my words.

"Unfortunately, I cannot," he replied. "The game must be played by the one who challenges it."

"FML," I muttered under my breath, feeling a cold sweat break out across my brow.

"Trust us, Alice," Hatter said softly, placing a reassuring hand on my shoulder. "We'll get through this."

"You know how clever I can be," Chess agreed, his sly grin widening. "Just follow our lead, and trust your instincts."

With a deep breath, I stepped onto the first square.

Almost immediately, a group of aggressive pawn chess pieces marched over to me, their jagged teeth bared menacingly as they blocked my path.

"Whoa, chill out, okay everyone?" I warned them, raising my hands in a peaceful gesture. "I'm not here to cause trouble. I just need to get across your board."

"Ha! Foolish girl!" the lead pawn snarled, its voice guttural and dripping with disdain. "No one crosses our battlefield without paying the price!"

"Then let us pay it," Hatter replied, his tone eerily calm. "What is it you want?"

"A worthy opponent . . . or your blood," the pawn sneered, and my heart leaped into my throat. "You decide."

"Charming," Chess remarked dryly, but I could see the excitement dancing in his eyes. This was a challenge he relished, and I started to feel that together, we could handle it.

"You have your teams," he said, motioning to the group of black pawns and the group of red ones. "We have ours. The three of us will be working together."

"Imbecile! There are only two sides in chess, not three!"

"Yes, but our team doesn't have enough players to fill the board," Chess told them. "What do you propose as a solution? We could have Alice move the pawns for the red team."

He motioned to the pile of red gravel and dust that the black pawn had recently killed. "What do you think of that idea? Red was already losing anyway. They must be unlucky today."

The pawns exchanged glances, their interest clearly piqued.

"Very well, you may play for the red side, but we're starting a new game," the lead black pawn said at last, its voice filled with skepticism. "Be warned, Alice. If you fail, we will tear you limb from limb."

"Can you at least start with my head so I don't feel any pain?" I asked, only half joking.

"No."

I rolled my eyes.

What a dick move.

"I guess we'll just have to kick all their asses," I told Chess and Hatter. Their confident gazes met mine without flinching. "We can do this, right, guys?"

"If you play your cards right," Hatter snickered under his breath.

Chess grinned wide at me, then faded into nothingness.

"I'm the luckiest one of all," he crooned into my ear. Even though I couldn't see him, I could feel his hands rest on both of my hips. "Come now, dear. Let me get you into position."

Ignoring me as took my place, the black and red pawns all moved back to their original spots on the giant board. Even the crumbled red one put itself back together and ran back to its square.

"Your move," said the lead pawn.

I turned to where Hatter was standing at the edge

of the board. Chess was still invisible, although I felt his presence. I took a deep breath and braced myself for the challenge ahead.

"Alright, guys . . . what do I do?"

"Move your pawn forward two squares," Chess instructed from somewhere off to my left side. His voice was low and measured.

"Which one are you talking about?" I asked, my eyes darting nervously between the pieces. "Aren't they all pawns?"

"Only the ones in the front row are called pawns," he replied. "Take one from the center and move it two places forward."

"Okay . . . here goes nothing." I took a deep breath as I guided the pawn forward. To my relief, the chess piece moved without any resistance, gliding obediently into its new position.

"Good," Chess praised, his green eyes gleaming with approval. "Now, let's see how black responds."

We watched our opponent make a similar move. Then it was our turn again.

"Left diagonal," Chess murmured after the black pawn stepped forward and drew a bow and arrow. With Chess coaching me, I was starting to feel a sense of exhilaration, like I was sneaking through enemy territory undetected.

"Three steps forward to the right," he advised. I hesitated for a moment, but then took the steps as directed.

As the opposing pieces shifted and changed, I struggled to keep up, my mind racing to find a pattern or strategy in their movements. But it was no use—I was hopelessly out of my depth, and I knew it.

"Move your knight," Chess said suddenly, his voice urgent. "To the left, then forward."

“Which one’s the knight?” I asked, starting to panic.

“The horse. Move it left, then forward.”

"Like this?" I asked, hesitating as I reached for the piece.

"Exactly," he replied encouragingly.

But as my fingers brushed against the cold, hard surface of the knight, I felt a sudden jolt of panic shoot through me, and I stumbled, accidentally knocking the piece into the path of an enemy pawn.

My heart caught in my throat as I realized I’d made a fatal mistake.

The chess pieces stopped their battle and turned their menacing gazes upon me. Fear gripped my chest as the monstrous figures advanced, their swords and bows drawn, their intentions clear—

capture or kill.

"Watch out!" Hatter shouted from the sidelines, his eyes wide with horror as the pawn lunged towards me, its razor-sharp sword drawn and gleaming.

“Oh, FUCK!” I shrieked, leaping back behind my chess piece, using it as a shield as a handful of arrows shot past me.

But it was too late. I’d taken a hit to my shoulder. It wasn’t very deep, but it was serious enough to make me start bleeding.

"What do I do?"

"Keep calm, Alice!" Chess urged, his voice tense with worry. "You need to counter their attack."

"How the fuck do I do that?" I cried, my mind reeling with fear and confusion as more arrows shot past me.

"Use your imagination—your instincts! You have it within your abilities to defeat them!"

"Could you be a little more specific?" I hissed through my clenched teeth.

My heart raced as the bloodthirsty pieces drew closer, but my mind was trapped in a whirlwind of panic. The chess piece I was hiding behind was impaled with dozens of arrows.

Pain was throbbing in my shoulder. Blood was dripping down the length of my arm and down one of my boobs.

Desperation clawed at my insides, my thoughts a tangled mess of fear and hopelessness.

"Move the bishop!" Hatter said.

"Are you sure?" Chess asked, his voice tainted with concern.

"Trust me," Hatter replied, his voice steady and confident. His gaze never left the violent game unfolding in front of us.

"Move the bishop, Alice. It's the piece with the funny hat.

Not knowing if this would be my last living memory or not, I tossed my bloody hair over my shoulder and moved the bishop where he told me to. I watched in awe as it swooped across the board, bludgeoned the threatening pawn to dust, and removed it from the board.

"Brilliant!" Chess exclaimed in such a way that I could practically hear his invisible hands clapping in delight. "Well done, Hatter, and well done, Alice!"

"Thanks," I replied, a fierce sense of pride swelling within me.

I may not have known how to play chess when this game began, but I was starting to figure out the different moves each piece was allowed to make. I was thinking up strategies and feeling more confident with each passing moment.

And as I stood there on that brutal chessboard, surrounded by darkness and danger, I knew that one thing was certain—I wasn't going down without a fight.

I had to be smarter, faster, more cunning than the chess pieces if we were to make it through this maze alive.

"Think, Alice," Hatter whispered, watching me closely. "What would you do if you were one of them?"

The words struck a chord within me, and something inside me snapped. Fury had ignited in my chest. The answer was so obvious, and I grinned wickedly as I realized what I should do.

Rules made no sense in Wonderland. This was a place where adorable, fuzzy pink bunnies were more deadly than piranhas. Flowers reeked of rotting flesh and the streams were thick with black muck.

Tea parties were thinly veiled orgies where the cake made you drunk and high. And the only demon I'd met hadn't hurt me. All he'd done was lick me to oblivion.

No . . . rules didn't matter at all here.

In Wonderland, rules were made to be broken.

The guys were constantly telling me to use my imagination.

Here went nothing.

Seizing the opportunity, I took a deep breath and focused my thoughts. I closed my eyes and I imagined the remaining chess pieces turning against one another.

I could feel the intensity of the pieces, their very souls yearning to move where I willed them to go. I opened my eyes to see theirs gleaming in rage, fixed on me, silently urging me to make a move.

I could see the hatred in their eyes, the way they longed to crush me beneath their feet. But I couldn't let that happen. I had to keep going, keep pushing my imagination to the limit.

Suddenly, in a flash of almost intangible power, the pieces came alive. I moved the kings and queens, pawns, rooks, knights, and bishops. One after another, the pieces captured each other just like I'd seen it happen in my mind.

The army of white went after white, and black descended on black in a frenzy of activity. They battled each other ferociously as I forced them into capturing each other in a twisted dance of carnage.

Dust and metal filled the air, clinking and

clanking as they collided with each other. Swords and shields clashed against metal and stone as they fought for dominance. The sound was deafening, but I didn't flinch. I had control over them now.

I continued to manipulate the pieces with my mind, moving them in a way that I had never thought possible. The knights leapt over the other pieces, the bishops diagonally sliced through their enemies, and the pawns pushed forward with newfound vigor.

It was as if my imagination had breathed life into the chess pieces, and they were now fighting for me.

The battle raged on for what felt like hours, but in reality, it was only a few minutes. It wasn't long before the once-imposing army began to fall apart, each piece exploding or breaking apart blow by blow.

And then, just as suddenly as it had begun, it was over.

The last piece fell to the ground with a resounding thud, and the once-deadly army was now nothing more than a heap of shredded metal and shattered stone.

I stood there, panting and shaking, but also exhilarated. I had never felt so alive. In that moment, I realized that I had tapped into something inside of me that I never knew existed before.

I was Alice, the woman who had conquered the impossible with nothing more than her imagination. And I knew that no matter what other terrors awaited me in Wonderland, I would face them with the same courage and determination.

"Checkmate, bitches," I panted, smirking at the dusty piles of carnage that lay crumbled on the board.

My legs trembled beneath my body, but I refused to give in to my exhaustion as the adrenaline wore off.

I couldn't give in.

I still didn't have the Vorpal Sword.

CHAPTER
ELEVEN
ALICE

Bloodied and breathing heavily, I staggered forward until I'd reached the other side of the weathered and worn chessboard. My long blonde hair was full of blood and my blue cocktail dress was torn and stained, clinging to me with my blood and sweat.

Every step felt like an eternity until I finally reached an enormous stone door. Its surface was etched with intricate symbols that seemed to shift and change when viewed from different angles.

Then the door opened with a slow creak to reveal a monster with a gaping mouth in the center, its jagged teeth bared in a sinister grin.

Luckily it was made of stone.

And unlike the chess pieces, it wasn't alive.

Thank fuck for that.

Inside the monster's huge mouth was a long, red velvet pillow where a tongue might've been. On that pillow sat a gleaming silver sword with a gold inlay and a fine golden cord woven around a black hilt. My heart thumped as I took it in.

"The Vorpal Sword," Chess purred as he sidled up to my right side.

"That's it?" I asked in disbelief. "We've finally found it?"

Yes. Very impressive, Alice," he nodded. "You're proving yourself to be quite the resourceful champion."

"You're more than simply resourceful. You are remarkable," Hatter breathed on my left, his brilliant blue eye shining down at me with admiration. "Truly, you are a force to be reckoned with."

"Thanks, guys," I replied, feeling a thrill of satisfaction course through me even as I winced at the pain in my battered body. I was bloody and sweating, covered in flakes of plant mud, but I was alive.

More importantly, I was growing stronger with every challenge I faced.

"Are you ready to take your prize?" Hatter asked. "You've certainly earned it."

"Alright . . . here goes nothing," I exhaled, my heart pounding in anticipation of retrieving the fabled weapon. My body was battered and bruised from our journey. All I really wanted was a hot bubble bath and a bucket of perfectly chilled champagne.

Even so, I couldn't help but feel a sense of excitement at the prospect of finally getting the sword. Once I had it, I could defeat that psycho bitch Red

Queen and her stupid Jabberwocky and restore balance to this demented realm.

Then I'd get my damned bubble bath.

"Before we proceed, you should know," Hatter began, his voice wavering slightly as he spoke, "neither Chess nor myself can physically retrieve the sword for you, Alice. It must be you who claims it. You and you alone."

"That figures," I scoffed, tossing my tangled blonde hair over my bloody shoulder.

I stepped forward and reached into the mouth for the sword, then saw a bright flash of blinding blue light. I was flung backwards so hard and so fast that I landed about ten feet behind the guys.

Hatter let out a low whistle as they rushed over to my side.

"What the hell just happened?" I groaned from the ground as they pulled me up to sit. The scent of ozone filled my nose, and my body hummed with electricity.

"It would seem that you touched a protective charm," Chess explained while helping me up to my feet.

"Holy fucking hearts and roses . . . I'd forgotten all about that," said Hatter while he curled an arm around my waist to keep me stable. "At least you didn't get hurt too bad."

"Define 'too bad,'" I growled from his side.

"You're still in one piece," Hatter explained. "That means you're not hurt too bad."

I begged to differ.

My left knee was killing me, and I'd scraped the shit out of my left hand and my left calf. I probably would've broken my ankle if I wasn't wearing the boots Chess had given me.

I stooped down and picked up one of the arrows that hadn't landed in my chess pawn shield from earlier. Then I limped over to the stone wall where the Vorpal Sword sat in the magical mouth.

Using the arrow like a pointer, I held the end with the feathers and carefully reached forward until the tip found the magical force field. Streaks of blue electricity sparked and zigzagged across the opening of the mouth, running over the entire surface of the shield.

My shoulders slumped as I stared hopelessly at the shimmering barrier. It seemed to hum with evil intent, and I realized there was no way I was getting through this thing.

Not unless I wanted to risk breaking every bone in my body. I was pretty sure I'd just fractured my kneecap.

I stood there clutching the arrow in my right hand, feeling the weight of defeat pressing down upon me, when a sudden glint in Hatter's eyes caught my attention. The laugh lines on his face seemed to smooth as a rare moment of pure clarity washed over him.

"Wait," he said, his voice calm and steady. "Alice, do you recall that riddle I told you during the tea party?"

I frowned, trying to summon the memory through the haze of debauchery and intoxication. I'd heard tons of riddles that night, but one in particular had burrowed into my thoughts, refusing to let go, because nobody had solved it.

"Is it the one about having a long, stiff shaft?" I asked offhandedly while I twirled the arrow in my fingers.

"That's the one," Hatter nodded, his gaze intense. "I remember now - the Vorpal Sword is held in place by a riddle spell. Solve the riddle, claim the sword. I tell so many riddles that I was afraid I'd forget which one would free the sword, so I wrote it down. Look."

Chess and I turned our heads to the stone doors where Hatter was pointing. The strange symbols pulsated and danced, then organized themselves into a single line.

"I have a long, stiff shaft," Chess read out loud. "My tip penetrates. I come with a quiver. What am I?"

"That's actually what it says up there?" I asked dubiously.

"It most certainly is," he replied. "That's the riddle that will free the sword."

"Of course!" Hatter exclaimed, his relief palpable. "That's probably why I told it to you in the first place! I just couldn't remember why I did because of, you know, being mad."

"Yeah, I get that," I told him, even though I could only relate from all the times I'd partied too hard and blacked out. "I suppose I should try a little harder to solve this riddle. Can you read it again, Chess?"

"I have a long, stiff shaft. My tip penetrates. I come with a quiver. What am I?"

My eyes flicked onto Hatter's mismatched ones.

"And you're absolutely *positive* that it's not a dick or a cock or a shlong or a penis of any kind?"

"It is not."

"Fuuuuuuuuck!"

I sank to the ground, realizing just how fucking tired I truly was.

"I guess I'll just sit here until I figure it out," I muttered, adjusting the straps of my bloodstained dress as I turned back to face the Vorpal Sword. My mind raced with possibilities, and I absentmindedly started using the arrow to dig a little hole in the ground as I thought about the riddle that had gone unsolved by me for days.

It had a long, stiff shaft.

The tip penetrates.

It came with a quiver.

And it wasn't a dick.

Or a cock.

Or a shlong.

Or a penis of any kind.

I was pissed off about my knee, about my shoulder, and annoyed about my dress. I'd been attacked not only by poisonous plants, but an entire chess board of crazy life-sized pieces that wanted nothing more than to kill me. I'd been fried by magic electricity and then drop-kicked.

And for some stupid reason, I'd picked myself up and come back for more.

Maybe I was just as mad as Hatter.

Maybe if I dug a big enough hole, I could crawl through it and leave Wonderland.

I started stabbing harder at the moldy soil, imagining myself crawling through the hole and ending up in that creepy old mansion that I'd followed Winston the White Rabbit to.

That night at the club seemed like another world away.

Technically, it was.

Even if this was still a dream.

What if it wasn't?

I'd find out where Dinah hid her stash of little blue pills and I'd take one to a private lab to have it analyzed so I could find out if she was actually drugging me with memory erasers that had the ability to hatch into fat worms.

For all I knew, Dinah was just giving me NyQuil to help me sleep better.

What if it wasn't?

What if Chess and Callister and Winston and Hatter were all right, and Dinah *wasn't* someone I could trust?

So far, none of my wicked boys of Wonderland had treated me in a way that made them untrustworthy. Callister was an asshole, but at least I understood his reasons why. Hatter was crazy, but in a good, super freaky way.

And Chess . . .

He acted like a gentleman, what with the tuxedo and the manners, but I had a feeling that he might be the biggest freak of them all.

I already knew he had a long, stiff shaft. I wondered what it would feel like the first time it penetrated me. I wondered if he'd stay in human form or be so overcome with sensation that he'd shift into some kind of monster demon when he came with a quiver deep inside of me.

I stole a glance at him, where he was chatting quietly with Hatter. His brilliant green eyes met mine, darkening with desire.

Unbelievable. Even though I was a fucking mess, he *still* wanted me.

He still hungered for me.

Still yearned for me.

"How are coming along?" he asked, his voice smooth as silk. "Are you getting close?"

"Not really," I said, jamming the arrow deep into the soft soil. It was going to take a while to dig all the way to Los Angeles.

"Pity," he said, tilting his head to one side, watching me dig. "I could've sworn the answer to the riddle was well within your grasp."

Hatter glared at him and backhanded him on the shoulder like Chess had just talked shit on his dear, sweet mom. The two of them started to bicker in hushed voices before Hatter dragged Chess away by his leopard print lapel.

Laughing to myself at their antics, I went back to digging. I shoved the arrow back into the soil even deeper this time, scratching out another handful of dirt.

Suddenly I stopped.

My hand curled around the feathered end of the long, stiff shaft, and I pulled the tip out of the soil, studying it up close. The tip was sharp and pointy. It wasn't meant to be a shovel. It was designed for the sole purpose of piercing.

Of penetrating.

"Guys?" I tentatively called out, my voice shaking with excitement as the answer hit me like a bolt of lightning. "I think I solved the riddle!"

I pulled myself onto my feet and walked back to the shimmering force field protecting the sword.

"The answer is an arrow!" I announced, feeling a burst of triumph surge through my limbs as the answer to Hatter's riddle clicked into place in my mind. "It's got a long, stiff shaft. The tip penetrates. And the container that holds arrows is called a quiver. That's the answer to the riddle, right?"

As the words left my lips, the air around me shifted. The constant stink of rot and mold was replaced with the soft fragrance of delicate flowers. The strange symbols on the huge stone door lit up and transformed into letters I could actually read.

I have a long, stiff shaft. My tip penetrates. I come with a quiver. What am I?

An arrow.

I approached the Vorpal Sword once more, and as I murmured the words of the riddle and its answer out loud, I felt an overwhelming surge of power course through me. That surge of power leaped from my body and into the gaping mouth of the stone Jabberwocky in front of me. A fan of tiny electrical sparks darted across the force field guarding the Vorpal Sword before exploding in a quick series of pops. The sword gleamed on the red velvet pillow where it sat, calling to me.

Beckoning to me.

With a deep breath, I reached out once more into the stone Jabberwocky's mouth and grasped the weapon. My hand wrapped confidently around the hilt, and this time, the sword came free with ease, its weight surprisingly light in my hand.

"Finally," I breathed, staring at the gleaming blade in awe. I could feel the strength of the weapon pulsating in my grasp, filling me with a newfound sense of purpose and determination.

My heart pounded in my ears as I took a step back and examined the sword closer. Even though I'd taken fencing classes for years, I'd never held such a substantial weapon. Fencing foils were thin, fine, and bendable. They were meant to do no harm.

The Vorpal Sword, however, was meant to slay.

And now it was in my hands.

I looked around for Hatter and Chess, but they'd vanished without a trace.

"Guys?"

My heart pounded harder.
"Guys? Where the hell are you?"
Nothing.
There was no reply at all.

CHAPTER
TWELVE
CHESS

Alice stood in the center of the clearing, the Vorpal Sword clutched in her hands as she examined the ancient runes etched along its blade.

Her blue dress was ripped at the seams and stained with blood and dirt. Her blonde hair was tangled around her face and pooling on her ample breasts in sweaty, blood-caked tendrils. She looked disheveled, exhausted, and utterly triumphant.

A surge of pride swelled in my chest and my cock at the sight of her.

Oh, Alice.

My clever, maddening mortal.

"Guys? Where the hell are you?"

Although I didn't enjoy hearing the undertones of concern in dear her voice, I absolutely relished how it made me feel for her to long for me.

To want me.

To *need* me.

As if she'd ever be rid of me now.

Oh no . . .

She might've had her pussy and her ass plundered by Hatter's cock, but my tongue had been there first. Licked her first. Filled her first.

Claimed her first.

Her ass might belong to Hatter, but that pussy was *mine*.

I hovered in the ether, invisible to them both, simply watching as Alice carried out her destiny.

She'd done it.

The darling creature had proven Callister wrong and successfully carried out her mission to retrieve the Vorpal Sword.

So what if I'd given her a little nudge in the right direction? I hadn't given her the answer to Hatter's riddle.

Not outright.

I'd merely guided her towards the place where she was already headed, then left her alone to figure it out.

Hatter stumbled into the clearing from behind the boulders where he'd been waiting and brushed a few leaves from his threadbare top hat. I materialized out of the ether, taking my human form.

The worry melted off of Alice's beautiful face as we came into her view. Her lips curved into a smile at the sight of us. Then she lifted up the Vorpal Sword in triumph.

Her prize was finally in her precious hands.

"Well done, Alice," Hatter sighed in relief, his

eyes shining with admiration. "That wasn't an easy riddle to solve. I knew you had it in you."

"I couldn't have done it without your help," she admitted, offering the weapon to me for inspection.

The runes on the blade were there for protection against harm, and I twirled the blade through my fingers with practiced ease.

In all my years of demonic existence, I'd held this weapon many times. Always with a different Alice. A young one. An innocent one. Neither the blade nor the girl were ever mine to keep.

No . . . the great game of destiny always dealt us the same cards.

First, the Red Queen's madness would put a chokehold on the Kingdom of Hearts and Roses. Her inner darkness would manifest into a Jabberwocky that terrorized all of her subjects into submission, until it spread to the borders of the Kingdom of Diamonds and Ice. Then the White Queen would summon the only champion who could defeat such evil—an innocent child.

An Alice.

Then I would introduce the girl to the way things worked in Wonderland. Callister would tease her . . . confound her. Use a fair bit of reverse psychology on her, because sometimes, when you tell a child they can't do something, it only makes them more determined to prove you wrong.

Then the Alice would use her innocence, her imagination, and the Vorpal Sword to destroy the Jabberwocky, essentially cutting out the rot from the

Red Queen's heart. She'd be relieved from all the wickedness in her soul, and Wonderland would go back to normal.

Alice would go home.

Then the cycle repeated.

It's the way things have always been.

I suddenly found myself hoping that this time—this Alice—would be different.

It already was.

Nobody had ever fucked an Alice before.

"We couldn't have done it without you, either," I said, letting my full Cheshire grin spread across my lips. "You never cease to amaze me."

Alice openly basked in our praise, the warmth of our words visibly chasing away the shadows of doubt that had plagued her ever since her arrival in Wonderland. I was looking forward to rubbing her success in Callister's face the next time we saw him.

"Aww, Chess . . . Did you think I'd let you down?"

My grip tightened around the hilt of the sword. Claiming the Vorpal Sword was merely the first step to ending the Red Queen's reign of terror. I knew we still had a long road ahead of us and countless challenges to overcome.

Best to take things one step at a time.

I didn't want to shake Alice's confidence now. Not when it was higher than it had been since she'd stepped into our world.

I shook my head, unable to keep from smiling at

her. "Never, darling. I never thought for one second that you'd let us down."

The longer I gazed at Alice, bloody and exhausted from all her efforts, the more I recognized the need for her to restore her powers.

She wasn't like us.

She didn't have Hatter's endless stores of fae energy, or my demonic ability to 'cat nap' and recharge in a fraction of the time it took her.

I conjured a scabbard and sheathed the Vorpal Sword near my hip, then gathered Alice into my arms.

"I knew all along that you could do it," I murmured softly while delicately stroking her filthy hair. Even spattered with blood and smeared with dirty sweat, her beauty could not be denied. "I think you've earned a reward for all your hard work."

"Yes, she certainly has," Hatter said. He sauntered closer to us, reaching beyond the barrier of my protective arms to take Alice's chin into his hand.

Ignoring me, he gazed at her with unapologetic lust, letting his thumb graze along her bottom lip. "You've proven yourself to be quite . . . capable. What would you like as a reward, Alice?"

From beneath the brim of his top hat, his mismatched eyes flicked over to mine. He smirked, then looked back at Alice.

"You could have *me*, if you like. Or you could have Chess. I know you told him to fuck you senseless once it was safe."

Alice shifted in my arms, letting out the softest of sighs.

I gazed down at her, quirking a brow in delight.

"Or . . . you could have us *both*."

Her breath hitched at my suggestion, and she bit her lip as she considered it, making me grin even more.

"We can give you nearly anything you could ever dream of," I murmured. "All you have to do is ask for it. Just say the words, Alice, and we'll give it to you."

"Oh, we definitely will," Hatter said with a wicked laugh.

Alice blinked in wonder at us both.

"Really?"

"Really. Just say it. Tell us what you want, and it's yours."

"Does it have to be only one thing?"

I laughed, then shook my head.

"No. Surely by now you know how generous we can be when it comes to you."

"Alright . . . " she said slowly, while her thoughts spun like the cogs in Winston's precious pocket watch. He was at the White Queen's court, waiting for us to show up with the Vorpal Sword and our newest Alice. She was supposed to begin her training with the White Knight, who would teach her how to defeat the Jabberwocky.

That's how it had always been done before.

But like I said earlier, this time was different.

This Alice was different.

Older.

Ripe for the fucking.

If I knew the White Knight, he was bound to teach her more than how to handle that sword.

If I knew Alice, she'd relish every second of it.

And while I truly didn't care *who* she fucked, I very much cared *when* she fucked them.

I'd explored the depths of her cunt before anyone else, but only with my tongue. I'd withheld my cock to keep her safe while she bounced on Hatter's as a consolation prize.

But I was determined to cram my length inside of her and drench her in my seed before she stepped foot in the White Queen's court.

I wanted my smell all over her. I wanted to mark her. To claim her.

To let everyone know that she was mine *first*.

Meanwhile, Alice's thoughts were moving so fast that I could only grasp a few snippets of what she wanted. I knew she wanted my cock. She wanted Hatter's as well, yet there was more on her mind than being stuffed from both ends.

She broke free from my arms, then walked back over to the clearing where she'd solved Hatter's riddle.

"I know what I want," she said with a coy grin while toying with her hair.

"Name it, and it's yours," I said, eyeing the swells of her curves with barely veiled hunger.

"I want a bubble bath," she declared. "And I want the water to have magic healing powers so that as soon as I get wet, I'm clean and all these cuts and bruises are gone. And I'd like some champagne on ice. Can you do that?"

"I can . . . " I replied with an obliging nod, trying to keep my disappointment and desire in check. Hatter nodded in agreement, his mismatched eyes twinkling with mischief, as if he knew we were both struggling to control ourselves around her.

It didn't take more than a moment for me to create a massive clawfoot tub filled with warm, fragrant water. Mountains of opalescent bubbles spilled over the edge, glittering from all the floating candles that hovered around. Their soft, amber light pushed back the darkness that was creeping in from all corners of the hedge maze, casting a warm, inviting glow over the scene.

Vines of flowers and plants surrounded the giant tub. The air was sweet with the scent of roses, jasmine, and other exotic blooms that seemed to be intoxicating.

Finally, I created a long bench to sit beside the tub, along with a sponge, a bar of the purple soap that she liked so much, a bucket of champagne on ice, and three glasses.

"Can I get in now?"

"Of course."

Before Hatter could offer to help her out of her clothes, she began to strip.

The shredded blue dress fell down her toned, tan legs and gathered around her ankles. Her filthy hair tumbled down her spine, luring our gaze to her gorgeous ass.

Her arms and legs and her shoulder were covered in bruises and battle wounds from the poisonous thorns and the deadly chess match.

I saw past it all.

Despite the damage, she was still so, so incredibly beautiful.

Hatter and I watched Alice climb into the tub and lower her battered body into the healing water. She held her nose and sank beneath the bubbles, disappearing from view for long enough that I grew concerned.

"Is she alright?" Hatter moved to the other side of the tub, scooping out one handful after another of bubbles to see where Alice had gone. They were so thick that it was useless.

Suddenly she burst up through the surface of the water, splashing us as she let out a gasp of exhilaration.

Despite the darkness and decay festering all around us, my precious mortal was more radiant than a hundred thousand stars.

From what I could see, there wasn't so much as a scratch left on her flawless body. All the blood and filth had vanished from her long, blonde hair cascading down her back. I could barely able to tear my eyes away. It shone in golden wet waves that spread across her breasts . . . then curled around her nipples.

I'd never been so envious of hair in all my existence.

"Feel better?" I asked, handing her a glass of champagne.

"Ohhh . . . fuck yeah. This feels so good, Chess . . . " she sighed in such wanton tones that it made me hard.

Hatter sat on the edge of the tub while I perched on the bench. Together we watched her swallow one greedy mouthful of wine after another.

I found myself wondering if she'd swallow my cock with as much enthusiasm once I finally let her see it. She might run away screaming. I lifted up my glass and smiled at Hatter, who was practically frothing at the mouth with restrained desire.

"Tell me," I said, leaning down close to her ear, "is there anything else you'd like now that you're healed? Anything else you desire?"

Alice hesitated for a moment, her blue eyes meeting mine, and then darting to Hatter's mismatched gaze. It was clear what she wanted, but would she have the courage to ask for it?

"There is . . . " She held out her glass for Hatter to refill it. Her eyes gleamed with amusement as she looked between us. She was a vision of loveliness and deadliness, like a rose with razor-sharp thorns."I want you both to get in here with me. I'm ready."

I smiled softly and shook my head.

"You might be ready for Hatter . . . but you're not ready for me."

"Yeah, I am," she insisted.

"No. You're not."

Alice scowled at me. Her disapproval grew even

deeper when she beckoned me to join her in the tub and I refused.

A primal flicker of pent-up tension tore through me at her reaction, and my demonic green eyes darkened.

"I will tell you when you're ready!" I growled through my bared teeth.

The little pinched frown on Alice's lips faded away. I thought she'd finally caught a glimpse of who—of *what*—she was dealing with, but her mouth simply curled into another one of her coy grins.

"Fine. Then you don't get to fuck me at all. You can just sit there and watch Hatter fuck me instead!"

Hatter let out a hearty laugh at my expense.

I wasn't amused.

A ball of dark energy swirled in the heart of my core, crackling through my veins. I narrowed my eyes and took a drink of champagne to mask the snarl of indignation on my face.

The girl was up to something.

Whatever game she was playing, I'd be the one to win it.

She had *no* idea who she was fucking with.

It wasn't a lie when I'd told her that sexual release would temporarily weaken my powers and leave us vulnerable to attack, but we were safe at the moment. I'd gladly take the opportunity to make good on my promise to fuck her senseless once the danger was gone.

However . . .

I was a Cheshire Cat demon. I was a ferocious,

hulking lion of a beast when in my truest form. If I fucked her before she was ready for me, it would tear her apart. Make her scream. Make her bleed.

It would make her hate me.

That was the very last thing I wanted.

"Fine," I replied with as much nonchalance as I could muster. Meanwhile, the dark ball of energy was flooding through my bloodstream, awaking all of my senses, preparing me to strike if she pushed me too far.

I channeled my magic towards the bathtub, splitting the walls and peeling them down like thick white flower petals. Hot foamy suds rode the water that rushed out in all directions.

With a flick of my wrist, I conjured a massive, thick mushroom cap to push out of the ground, essentially placing Alice at the center of a silky soft, cushioned platform. I surrounded it with even more floating candles that cast a warm, seductive glow upon the scene. A gentle breeze wafted through the air, carrying with it the sweet scent of flowers in full bloom.

"I *will* just sit here and watch Hatter fuck you instead," I told her from where I still sat on the bench. "I enjoy watching you come, after all. And he does enjoy having an audience. Don't you, my friend?"

"Very much so," Hatter snickered while slipping out of his shirt.

From the center of the mushroom, Alice jutted out her chin at me and frowned at my lack of compliance. It was obvious she wasn't used to having anyone tell her 'no.' It brought me great pleasure to deny her the satisfaction of giving in to her demands.

It gave me a little less pleasure to watch Hatter take off the rest of his clothes, climb onto the mushroom beside her, and slip his tongue past her lips, but there's something about being an immortal demon that few understand—

It makes us *incredibly* patient.

And I knew that when Alice was ready for me, it would all have been worth the wait.

I sipped champagne from my place on the bench while Hatter's hungry mouth explored Alice's gorgeous, naked body.

How *dare* she tell me—a demon!—to sit here and watch?

Lovely as she was, this Alice was spoiled.

Entitled.

Greedy.

Hatter wasn't enough for her, and we both knew it.

Alice knew, but wasn't admitting it.

She would.

Making her wait until she was begging for my demon cock would make her surrender to me even sweeter.

I trembled with excitement as I watched her wrap her arms and legs around Hatter's body. His mouth was on hers, his tongue stroking her own in a deep, searing kiss. His hands were busy kneading and squeezing her breasts until her pink nipples pebbled under his skillful touch.

"You taste so good," he murmured, pressing kisses along her neck and shoulders. He moved to her collarbone, kissing and nipping at the delicate flesh, drawing soft moans from her lips.

He flipped her onto her hands and knees, then spread her thighs apart, exposing her pussy and her ass to the open air.

Exposing them to me.

"Jealous?" he teased.

I shook my head, but inside I was raging.

I wanted to be the one spreading her, licking her . . .

Fucking her.

It wouldn't be much longer before she was begging for me to do all of those things.

All in good time.

Alice moaned and squirmed against Hatter's palm as he knelt down and sank his thumb into her slick heat, eliciting a cry of pleasure from her sweet lips.

"Exquisite," Hatter murmured, his mismatched eyes drinking in the sight of her as his tongue darted out to swipe across her dark orifice. She gasped, arching into the sensation, her hands clutching at the mushroom as his fingers massaged her clit.

"Hatter," she whimpered, spreading her knees in silent invitation as he continued his exploration of her body. "I need more."

He buried his face in her ass, delivering long

strokes interspersed with sliding his tongue and fingers into her hole. Alice let out a whimper, backing into his face, into his hand, pressing against his fingers until they rubbed out a soft, sweet orgasm. I watched her hole tighten with gentle contractions as she moaned into the night air.

"Hatter, I need you to fuck me," she demanded. "Fuck my pussy!"

"You'd better not come in that pussy," I warned him. Driven mad with lust, my demon was bordering near the edge of insanity. Hatter was my friend since time immemorial, but if he filled her cunt with his seed before I did, I might just tear him to shreds.

A wicked grin spread across Hatter's face as he glanced at me.

"Maybe I won't fuck it at all," he mused as he stroked himself. His other hand curled around the back of Alice's neck, drawing her face to his crotch. "Let's see how well your sassy little mouth takes my cock."

As Alice took him into her mouth, her eyes locked on mine. The sight of her warm, wet lips enveloping another man nearly drove me over the edge, but I held back, determined to savor every moment of our debauchery.

Her eyes never leaving mine, I could practically feel the ache that was consuming her body. I knew what she really wanted . . . what she craved . . . and she was finally coming around to accepting that she'd made a mistake in banishing me to the bench.

The anticipation of having her wrapped around

me was driving me mad, but all I did was slip off my jacket and drink another glass of champagne.

"Such a pity she said you couldn't fuck her," Hatter taunted while continuing to thrust into her throat. "Spread your legs so Chess can see how bad you want him to fuck you. Go on and be a good girl."

Alice's eyes fluttered, but she obediently reached behind her back and spread her inner lips apart. A slick sheen of desire was drenching her inner folds.

I clenched my jaw and curled my fingers into the bench feeling my nails dig into the wood.

"Do you see that? Look how wet she is!" Hatter laughed in between the occasional groan. "What do you think, Alice? Would you rather have Chess watching you . . . or fucking you?"

"Mmmmphhh."

He pulled out of her mouth and gazed down at her.

"Say it so he can understand you."

I watched her mouth press into a flat line before casting me an embarrassed look.

"I'd rather have him fucking me," she admitted.

Slowly, ever so slowly, my Cheshire Cat grin spread across my face. I rose to my feet.

"Are you sure, Alice?" I asked, wanting her to be certain of her desires.

"Yeah," she replied, determination lacing her voice. "Trust me, I've had plenty of time to think about it."

"Then it would be my pleasure," I purred, my fingers running through my dark hair as I stepped onto the giant mushroom. "But I have to warn you . . . I'm not made like other men."

With a flick of my wrist, I sent the last of my clothes flying across the garden, proudly displaying my impressive organ for Alice to see.

She bit her lip, her gaze fixed on my cock, an expression of bewildered, yet lustful curiosity on her face.

It was longer than any mortal man's, and its girth was formidable. The head was flared, almost like that of a snake, and the shaft was covered in ridges and bumps designed for maximum pleasure.

Alice's eyes widened at the sight of me . . . at the size of me, and I could see both fear and intrigue simmering just below the surface of her lovely blue orbs. The thrill in her eyes was unmistakable, but there was also a hint of trepidation that I found endearing.

"Oh, Chess," she breathed, reaching out to touch it hesitantly. "I thought it would be sharp, but it's . . . it's . . . it's so . . . *different*."

"Darling, I am a demon after all," I reminded her with a sly smile, pleased by her fascination. "And I assure you, its uniqueness is *entirely* to your benefit."

CHAPTER THIRTEEN

ALICE

A thrill of fear and excitement ran through me as I eyed Chess's huge, freakishly shaped dick. It was equally scary and fascinating, creating a heady concoction inside me that flooded my veins with anticipation.

After waiting all this time to know what fucking a demon would be like, I knew wanted to feel that monster cock inside me, stretching and filling me . . .

But *how*?

"You really think that thing's going to fit inside me?" I asked him with a skeptical frown.

"I do," he rumbled, dipping his chin. He reached forward and hooked his hands around the back of my knees, then dragged my ass to the edge of the giant mushroom. "We'll work our way up to it."

Heat scorched my cheeks even as wetness pooled between my legs.

Hatter chuckled behind me, his hands gliding down my arms. "She's not as naive as she seems, this one." His hard cock pressed into the small of my back, hot and insistent. "I think she'll take you just fine. I think she can take us both, if you play your cards right."

"That shouldn't be a problem for our lucky little Ace of Spades," Chess purred, sliding effortlessly between my legs. "We'll go slowly. Make sure you're ready in every way."

"So beautiful," Hatter breathed as he knelt down beside me. He ran a hand down my side, over my hip, along my leg. "And all ours."

"Yes. All ours," Chess agreed in a low purr that felt like velvet on skin. Completely captivated by their possessiveness, shivers raced over me and I was suddenly aware of the fact that they *were* truly mine. They were mine and I was theirs, and together we would explore pleasures I'd only ever dreamed of before now.

Chess took advantage of this moment to swoop in and claim my mouth with his own, his tongue tangling with mine while his hands roamed across my body in greedy exploration.

The soft surface of the mushroom gave way as they shifted. Hatter released my nipple to trail kisses over my ribs and stomach while Chess moved lower, his fingers splaying over my hipbones, his mouth finding the inside of my thigh.

I shuddered, caught between them both. My breathing was growing faster in anticipation of what my wicked boys of Wonderland were about to do to me.

The smell of sex was heavy on the air now. I could smell myself reacting to their touch as their four skillful hands roamed my body. I'd never felt the sensation of two tongues licking me, or two mouths kissing me.

I wondered how I'd made it this far in life without knowing what I was missing. I didn't just want my wicked boys—I *needed* them like I needed air to breathe.

I wouldn't be satisfied until they'd wrung every ounce of ecstasy from my body and left me limp and exhausted in their arms.

"So wet already," Chess murmured in approval, his fingers sliding through my folds to circle my entrance. "So ready for us."

"Good girl," Hatter praised while stroking my hair. "Let me fuck your mouth again while Chess fucks you with his."

"Wha—" I began to ask, but was promptly silenced by Hatter's dick being shoved past my lips. I welcomed the intrusion of his hard, smooth heat. The salty sweetness of him filled my mouth, and I sucked on him like I expected his cum to taste like champagne.

I groaned as Chess's demon tongue unfurled and plunged into my pussy, flexing and thickening against my inner walls. I moaned on Hatter's cock as the fullness of him spread through me.

"Fuck!" I cried out around my mouthful of cock. "Oh, fuck!"

Hatter hissed as my teeth caught on the head of

his cock, but it only made him fuck my mouth deeper. Chess's tongue began to thrust in and out of me faster . . . harder. The silky, rough texture was rasping against my clit.

I was so wet, I could feel my juices trickling down my legs and my ass, making a slick, wet spot on the mushroom, but Chess ignored it as he greedily fucked me with his tongue.

Taste me, I thought as I caught his gaze.

Drink me.

With each thrust of his smooth, wet, meaty muscle, I felt myself getting closer and closer to the edge of orgasm. I moaned again, my eyes rolling back in my head as I began to lose myself to the euphoria.

All around me, the world was reduced to a hazy cloud of sensation and sound. I didn't know when Hatter had grabbed my hair in both of his hands and started fucking my throat, and I didn't care. All I knew was that I was surrounded by hot, hard, gorgeous dick, and I couldn't get enough of it.

Hatter's grip tightened on my hair, pushing my head deeper onto his shaft with each stroke of his hips. My body shuddered and quaked with pleasure until he groaned and filled my mouth with his salty-sweet cum. The moment I swallowed it, I instantly felt a craving for more.

"Good girl," he sighed, giving my mouth a few more thrusts as he drained his balls onto my tongue. I sucked him clean, feeling strangely empty when his dick slipped out of my mouth. "Oh, Alice . . . I've never felt anything so spectacular! You're incredible."

I was so close to coming I could smell it. I could feel the electricity of a massive orgasm rising inside of me, coiling tight and waiting to snap. All I needed was one more thing, one more sensation, and I would explode.

I wanted Hatter to pinch my nipples. Play with my ass. Bite my neck.

"You want it, Alice?" he asked. "You want to come for us?"

"Yes . . . " I moaned.

"I don't think you mean it. Say it like you want to come for us."

"I wanna come for you!" I begged. "I wanna come so bad!"

"Do you want to get fucked, Alice?" he asked, sharing a glance with Chess before turning his attention back to me. "You want to get fucked by us?"

"Yeah," I whimpered.

"Say it," he urged. "Tell us how bad you need to get fucked."

"I need it!" I gasped. "I need to get fucked so bad!"

"Are you ready for Chess to fuck you with his huge, thick demon cock?" Hatter asked. "Will you be a good girl for us and come on his cock?"

"Fuck yes!" I pleaded. "Give it to me!"

Chess's fat, wet tentacle tongue rolled back into his mouth and he dragged me to the center of the soft mushroom.

My body trembled with excitement as he pinned me down to the mushroom, his face mere inches from mine. Every nerve in my body lit up. The look in his brilliant green eyes was dark.

Feral.

Possessed.

His knees split my legs apart, spreading them wide, and then I felt the tip of his huge, bulbous, freakishly shaped cock nudging between my pussy lips. My clit was throbbing for friction. My pussy was aching to be fucked.

I tilted up my hips, offering myself to my Cheshire Cat.

"Fill me," I whispered to him. "Fuck me."

Hot, wet, thickness spread me so wide that it burned, the size of his cock overwhelming me as he pushed inch by inch towards my core. His cock was bigger than anything I had ever felt before and it filled me up completely, pushing and stretching me in delicious ways. I winced in pain, then in pleasure as the ridges on his shaft massaged my G spot.

"Oh, fuck! I'm gonna come!" I groaned. "I'm not ready!"

"I say you're ready," he grinned, thrusting deeper, harder. The knobs and ridges stretched me wider and filled me until I thought I might burst.

I lifted my head to watch his giant monster cock fuck my pussy, and I gulped in disbelief.

He was only halfway inside.

With each stroke, every heated plunge of his body, it sent me higher and higher until I couldn't take anymore. Being stretched, getting fucked, the ridges massaging even harder, faster, hotter—it was all too much. I spiraled into a mind-shattering orgasm that shook my entire being.

I cried out into the night, gulping lungfuls of air as ecstasy washed over me in thick, heavy waves.

"Ohhh, very good, Alice," crooned Hatter from behind me. "Let's see if you can do that again . . . this time with his entire length inside you."

I shook my head.

"There's no way . . . " I panted. "I'm not ready."

"I say you're ready," Chess replied, flexing his cock inside me.

The mushroom vibrated underneath us, pushing up behind Chess. He grasped my hips and lifted me up until we were sitting in a cushioned chair made of the firm, yet squishy mushroom cap.

I was straddled on top of him at a slightly reclined angle, giving me a perfect view of his rippling abs. His body was like hot skin stretched over hard steel. I let my eyes wash over his perfection, thinking he couldn't get any better.

Then, he did.

Above the neck of his cock, an eruption of bumps and ridges broke out, perfectly placed like a little runway for me to rub my clit against.

My eyes widened.

With a satisfied grin, Chess reached down and wiped up some of the juice that I'd leaked all down his shaft. Then he spread it over the textured flesh, turning it into a nubby slip & slide for my clit.

"Ohhhh . . . ." I gasped. Was that meant for what I thought it was?

Yes. Yes it was.

I want.

I *need.*

"You wanted to fuck me?" he asked, grinning as he lifted a black brow at me. "Then fuck me."

I tossed my hair and grasped his shoulders with renewed determination. Come hell or high water, I was going to work his dick all the way in so I could feel that sensation on my clit.

Chess rested his hands on my hips, guiding me down, pulling me closer to him. It burned and stung, but the ridges on his shaft soothed the pain just enough to make me keep going. I shuddered in pleasure as I felt more of his thick, ridged demon cock work its way deeper inside me.

The nubs and ridges above his cock were calling to my clit, begging me to rub myself against them. I was desperate to do just that, so I leaned back a little and started to bounce up and down on him, faster and faster. My clit started to swell in anticipation.

I felt those bumps and ridges getting closer.

Closer.

And then I felt them dancing all over my clit.

Just a whisper at first.

Then a little more pressure.

Then even more.

Hot, slick stimulation made me spread my legs even wider. Made me tilt my hips and grind against Chess's body, using him for my pleasure.

Fucking him.

Riding him like a fucking hobby horse.

I let out a moan of pleasure as I felt Chess start to thrust in time to my bouncing and grinding. His thick, ridged demon cock sank deep into my pussy, giving me everything I wanted. His shaft was like an infernal furnace, forming itself to the contours of my body and releasing pulses of burning desire with each thrust.

Every time he filled me deeper and faster, I was able to rub myself harder against the small nubs and ridges that ran along his shaft, sending shockwaves of ecstasy rippling through me.

Hatter's mouth was sucking on one of my nipples now, while he reached around my back and worked a wet finger worked its way into my ass. With each swirling motion of his tongue and his finger, it felt like my entire being was about to be unraveled.

Chess captured my mouth in a passionate kiss, deepening our connection before either of us could surrender to the growing heat within. He was a demon, a creature of the night—not of darkness, but of fire and passion.

I wanted to set him on fire.

I wanted to make him come for me.

Chess had other plans.

"Do you want to fuck her pussy?" he asked Hatter. "She won't be so tight after I'm finished with her."

Suddenly my body was pulled backwards as Hatter held me against his chest and mounted me from behind.

"I don't care if he *does* destroy your pussy," he

growled in my ear. His balls slammed against me, wet skin hitting wet skin. "It's your ass that belongs to me. Now lean forward like a good little slut and suck his dick while I fuck you."

Hatter's hand pushed down on my back, and I braced myself on Chess's knees, sucking and licking and bobbing my head in time with Hatter's relentless thrusts. My clit was throbbing for attention, so I reached down to touch myself.

Chess's hand immediately grabbed my wrist, pulling it up to his cock, making my fingers curl around his shaft and stroke him while I sucked.

"You don't come until I say you can."

I whimpered on his shaft, navigating the ridges and bulbous shapes with my tongue.

Meanwhile, Hatter pulled out his dick, making me almost cry in misery.

I felt so empty without him.

"Keep sucking," Hatter ordered. "I'm not finished fucking you."

My lips and tongue went back to work on Chess, but I gasped and choked on his cock when I felt Hatter's crown pressing into my ass. He was so lubed up from pounding my dripping pussy that it was easy for him to burrow into my tight channel.

He let out a hiss of pleasure as he sank balls-deep into my ass. And as much as I loved the strange sensation of Chess's cock in my mouth, I wanted him back in my cunt.

He belonged there.

I moaned, unable to form words, wanting nothing

more than to drown in these dark delights. I wanted to be devoured by the bodies of the men giving themselves to me. My madman and my demon.

What more could a girl want?

I had ideas.

Time to use my words.

"Chess," I gasped as I lifted my head from his throbbing dick, "I want . . . I need more."

Chess's eyes sparkled with an insatiable hunger.

He'd liked what he'd heard.

"What did you have in mind?" he asked, a wicked grin spreading across his face.

"I want you both inside me . . . at the same time."

My slutty, greedy heart raced at the thought as Chess shared a heated glance with Hatter.

"How does a good girl ask for that?" Hatter asked while continuing to fuck my ass.

"Please," I shuddered.

Chess looked at me like he didn't believe me. Hatter stopped fucking and slipped out of my body.

I felt so empty.

I wanted to cry.

"Are you sure you want us both at the same time? It will be unlike anything you've ever experienced."

I nodded, my resolve unwavering. "I trust you both. Please? I want you to make me feel whole."

With that, Chess helped me back onto his lap. Hatter positioned himself behind me, his large cock nudging at the entrance of my ass.

"Don't forget to breathe," Hatter whispered, gently pushing forward. My eyes widened with a mix of pleasure and pain. I groaned in relief as he slid inch by inch into my tight passage.

As Hatter began to thrust slowly, Chess guided the head of his swollen shaft to my wet opening. The sensation of my pussy gripping him as he entered me sent shivers down my spine.

"Fuck . . . you guys . . . " I groaned, my body trembling as their cocks stuffed me to the brim. Chess purred at the expression of sheer wonder plastered on my face.

"How does it feel?"

I panted, trying to force my brain to remember words.

"It feels incredible to be filled so completely," I admitted.

"Good. Now relax, darling," Chess murmured, beginning to rock his hips in slow rhythm with Hatter's. "Soon you'll crave this feeling."

I took a deep breath and let it out.

Then another.

"'That's it, Alice," Hatter crooned from behind. "Just relax and enjoy yourself."

I enjoyed the shit out of it. Every brush of their hands, every slide of their bare skin against mine as they moved to surround me, the warmth of their mouths and the heady scents in the air, all combined into a perfect storm of pleasure threatening to drown me in ecstasy.

"We're going to make you feel so good," Chess murmured in my ear before claiming my mouth in another one of his scorching kisses.

The kiss pulled me against his stomach, rubbing my clit against those warm, nubby ridges on his body.

My sighs morphed into animalistic grunts of pleasure, and I fucked and bucked a little harder, struggling and failing to maintain control.

Hatter let out a wicked laugh, and Chess's fingers felt like claws digging into my hips.

"I think she's ready for us to fuck her now."

My eyes snapped open.

"You're already fucking me!" I pointed out in bewilderment.

They shook their heads.

"This isn't fucking."

"It's not?"

"No. This is us getting warmed up."

I sucked in a sharp breath, trembling.

Waiting.

In perfect unison, they thrust deep into me, breaching the depths of my tight holes in one smooth glide after another. I screamed, the sound echoing into the night, as the three of us began to move as one. They pounded into me with such primal hunger that I knew they planned to ruin me for anyone else.

Mine, the word echoed through my mind with every snap of their hips.

Ours.

Always.

A broken sob escaped my lips, but whether from pain or pleasure, I couldn't tell.

It was all the same to me.

And I didn't care. All that mattered was the slick

heat filling my holes, and the knowledge that I belonged to them.

Chess and Hatter set a punishing pace, reveling in the way my body stretched to accommodate them, my inner walls clenching down as if to trap them inside me. Chess matched Hatter thrust for thrust, their cocks sliding against each other through the thin wall separating my passages.

The lewd sound of flesh slapping flesh filled the air, punctuated by my groans and cries and the sounds of insects and tree frogs humming in the night. I leaned forward, bracing myself on Chess's body until he grasped my hair and yanked my head back, baring the long line of my throat.

Hatter leaned forward, his lips and teeth biting and kissing the tender flesh of my neck until he found my mouth and plunged his tongue next to mine, kissing me with savage hunger.

I trembled between them, writhing as much as their bodies allowed, torn between escape and surrender.

"Please," I gasped when Hatter released my lips. "Please, I can't—it's too much—"

"Shh," Chess soothed, even as he pistoned into me without mercy. "Just feel, Alice. Feel us claiming you, marking you as ours forever."

Hatter chose that moment to bite the back of my neck.

"Chess . . . Hatter . . . " I gasped out, feeling the coil of pleasure tightening within me, threatening to snap at any moment. "I'm so close . . . "

"Let go, Alice," Hatter urged, his voice low and rough as he quickened his pace. "We're right here with you."

I stiffened, my back arching away from Hatter's abdomen as a wail was torn from my throat.

Hatter groaned in approval.

"Yes, that's it. Ride it out, Alice. Don't fight it. Just let it take you away and enjoy the ride."

I closed my eyes and relished the sensation of being so completely stretched and filled. I could feel every inch of them inside me, and it felt both delicious and painful at the same time. I moaned with unhinged pleasure as they continued to thrust in and out of me.

The added pressure of Chess's ridges and nubs rubbing on my clit was too much. With one final, desperate cry, I shattered, my vision going white as my body spasmed around them. My walls clamped down on my wicked boys like a vise, rippling in the throes of my climax.

My pussy and my ass clenched both of their cocks, squeezing and milking them with such force that Hatter came within seconds of me. I felt my ass fill up with his warm cum, felt my heart explode with joy at hearing his moans of satisfaction.

I'd done that to him.

Me.

Made him come so hard, so deep in my ass.

I wanted to do the same thing to Chess.

I wanted all of what they had to give me.

I wanted to fucking *drain* them . . . make them mine.

I twisted and bucked against them, wrenching out every last drop of cum from Hatter until he shuddered and pulled his dick out of me.

The second he dismounted, Chess shoved him aside and pushed me to the ground, then lined up behind me. He thrust his entire length deep into my pussy, pounding mercilessly until I felt his cock swell even more.

Then more.

I didn't think it was possible.

I howled as he anchored himself deeper than I thought possible.

He came with such a ferocious roar that it shook the trees around us, throttling me with a powerful spasm that ripped another orgasm from within.

I mewled and thrashed like a bitch in heat as he blasted my insides with his thick ropes of cum. I arched my back, hungry for more, savoring the sensation as he pumped stream after stream of burning seed into my greedy pussy.

The feeling of his orgasm rippling through me was nearly unbearable, and I reveled in every second of it. A hot, slippery trail of his cum spilled out of me and coated my thighs as he pumped every last drop of his cum into me.

Utterly exhausted and covered in a sheen of sweat, I collapsed on my stomach. Every nerve in my entire body was buzzing and humming with approval.

When he pulled out, I pouted and groaned, aching to be filled again, but grateful to be their little cum slut. Every trickle that seeped out of me was a testament to the fact that they'd claimed me.

"I take it you're satisfied?" Chess murmured as he curled up beside me. Hatter crawled over and lay down on my other side, lazily caressing my skin.

"Mmm hmm . . . " I nodded. "I could die happy right now."

"Please don't do that," he said after a wide yawn. "You still have work to do."

"We'll leave for the White Queen's court first thing in the morning," Hatter said. He reached over and grabbed the edge of the mushroom cap, pulling it over the three of us like a thick blanket. "But first we sleep."

"I'm not sleepy," I protested.

Hatter's mismatched eyes twinkled with intrigue. "Neither am I, but Chess needs time to recover. He'll be completely useless until this time tomorrow."

"Not completely useless," muttered Chess, although I wasn't convinced. His eyes were closed, but he still had a soft grin on his face.

"You drained all your magic," Hatter pointed out. "That makes you useless to me."

"Not completely useless," Chess repeated. He draped a muscular arm around me, pulling me closer to his body. "I can keep Alice warm."

"Fine," Hatter conceded. "You keep her warm. I'll keep her company."

"Be my guest. She's both of ours, after all."

Hatter looked at me, his eyes burning with desire, and I arched my back, pressing my ass against his cock. He could have his choice of where he put it. I just didn't want to be empty any longer than necessary.

"Fuck me to sleep?" I asked. He took his cock in his hand and stroked himself fully erect, rubbing against the sticky cum still weeping out of me.

"How does a good girl ask?"

"Please."

"Very good, Alice," he sighed, then pushed himself into me for one more ride.

Yes. Oh yes. This was *exactly* what I needed. What I'd always craved without knowing. Without being bold enough to even ask.

I couldn't believe I'd ever thought Remy was good enough for me. Him and his boring, basic, cheating little human dick were just a blip in my sexual history. After being with my Mad Hatter and my Cheshire Cat, I'd never want anyone else.

They'd done exactly what they said they'd do.

They'd claimed me.

They'd ruined me.

And I loved it.

CHAPTER
FOURTEEN
ALICE

I dreamt I was lifted into a pair of strong arms and carried somewhere safe in a blanket covered in thick red and white stripes.

"Shhh..." a voice whispered. "Go back to sleep, Alice."

Chess must've regained enough of his strength for us to start making our way to the White Queen's court. How sweet and thoughtful of him to let me rest while he carried me. I was so completely spent from all the fucking that I wasn't sure my legs would work even if I'd wanted them to.

Without opening my eyes, I nuzzled into the warm shoulder and drifted back to sleep.

I woke up to find myself surrounded by black.

The room smelled like smoke and cherries. It was bathed in a warm golden glow, emanating from an array of black candles that flickered seductively around the space. Black velvet curtains had been pulled across the windows, blocking out all the light from outside.

The walls and the ceiling were lined with mirrors in ornate golden frames. They seemed to move and pulse with a life of their own.

I rubbed my eyes, feeling my body shift on black satin sheets and matching black satin pillows. Someone had put me in a simple, yet elegant black silk gown.

I'd fallen asleep naked outside on a mushroom and woken up in what looked like a luxury hotel suite.

Talk about an upgrade.

The floor was made of polished black and gold tiles that appeared to be simultaneously solid and liquid, rippling beneath my feet as I stepped off the bed and into a pair of fuzzy black slippers.

Despite its opulence, the room was oddly welcoming, and the bed beneath me felt far more comfortable than it had any right to be. There was even a faint scent of roses lingering in the air, as if daring me to let my guard down.

A soft sound caught my attention—the rustle of cards being shuffled. My gaze snapped to a nearby table where Callister and an elegantly dressed dark-haired man lounged on a black velvet sofa, pink smoke gently swirling in the air above them. The man's fingers deftly shuffled and manipulated a deck of playing cards before dealing himself and Callister a hand.

I couldn't see his face, but a gleam of gold got my

attention. The candlelight had caught on a gold pinky ring on his left hand.

I knew what pinky rings meant.

It meant Callister's friend thought he was hot shit.

We'd see about that.

"Good morning, Alice," Callister drawled, not even bothering to look up from his hand of cards. His tattoos peeked out from beneath the sleeves of his black leather jacket, making him look even more devilishly handsome than usual. They seemed to shift and dance beneath the dim candlelight, and the cherry tobacco scent filling the room could only be coming from the cigarette caught between his lips.

"Where am I?" I demanded, my voice cracking slightly despite my best efforts to sound chill as fuck. "What's going on?"

"Ah, Alice," Callister said with a wicked grin, finally looking up at me. "Let me introduce you to the King of Clubs. He's the one you can redirect your questions to."

The dark-haired man rose to his feet and headed my way, never letting his piercing gaze leave my face.

Well, one thing was for certain.

The guy *was*, in fact, hot shit.

He was almost as tall as Hatter, clad entirely in black, from his impeccably tailored three-piece suit to his polished shoes. His vest was adorned with gold embroidery and a gold pocket square peeked out of his jacket. In the dim light, I could see the emblem of a gold club pinned to his lapel.

He looked like a dangerous sort of royalty, with high cheekbones and a sharp jawline that could cut glass. His ebony hair fell over one eye, and a smirk played on his lips like he knew a secret he'd never share.

"The gown suits you," he said, unapologetically eyeing my curves while motioning for me to turn in a circle for him.

I did no such thing.

"It's alright," I muttered sarcastically, scanning the stranger for any signs of malice as he approached me.

His dark eyes were cold and calculating, yet undeniably attractive.

"You can always take it off if you don't care for it," he quipped. "I don't think Callister would mind."

My eyes darted over to where Callister still sat on the black velvet sofa.

"I wouldn't mind."

I ignored him, but my cheeks flushed deep pink. I could tell because I caught my reflection in one of the dozen mirrors hanging around the room.

"Why am I here?" I asked again. The king started to play with the cards in his hand.

"We'll discuss that after our guest has left," he replied.

I wrinkled my forehead in confusion.

"*Our* guest?" I asked. "What's that supposed to mean?"

"It means you belong to me," said the king.

"Is this some sort of sick joke?" I demanded, my

hands balling into fists. "Did you make some kind of deal with him, Callister?" The thought of betrayal stung, especially after everything we'd been through together.

Callister looked up from his cards, meeting my gaze with a shrug. "Sometimes, Alice, you have to play the hand you're dealt."

"Such wisdom," the King of Clubs said with a smirk. "But it's true. We all have our own games to play, and sometimes we must align ourselves with unexpected allies."

"Even if it means betraying your friends?" I spat, my chest tightening at the thought of Callister selling me out to this sinister figure.

"Ah, Alice," said Callister, laughing to himself as he drew on his cherry tobacco cigarette. "Always so full of spirit."

"Yes," the king agreed with a nod. "It's almost a shame, really."

"What's a shame?" I demanded.

"It's almost a shame I'll have to break you."

"Break me?" My heart did back-to-back somersaults at hearing those words. "Just what the hell are you planning to do with me?"

A vicious gleam filled the king's fathomless eyes.

"Oh, you'll learn soon enough once our guest leaves."

I swallowed hard, trying to focus my thoughts, trying to remain calm. It wasn't going to do any good to start screaming when I was trapped in a room with two powerful men who didn't seem to be human at all.

"Where are Chess and Hatter?" I asked, trying to keep my voice steady.

The king shrugged.

"Probably wherever the Tweedles left them."

Again, I furrowed my brow in confusion.

"The Tweedles?"

"His henchmen," Callister answered before taking a long drag off his cherry cigarette. He gave one puff and a canvas of white smoke filled the space in front of him. He gave another, and a row of thick red stripes bled down the white smoke.

My heart pounded in my chest as I recognized the red and white stripes from the blanket in my dream. It hadn't been a dream at all.

They'd taken me.

The King of Clubs had sent the Tweedles to kidnap me. I had no idea what had happened to Hatter and Chess, but I needed to find out. I couldn't shake the feeling that something was very, *very* wrong.

"Are they safe?" I asked, feeling my mouth go dry.

The King of Clubs chuckled softly, revealing a set of unnervingly sharp canine teeth.

"Don't worry about them right now, dear Alice."

His dismissive tone sent a shiver down my spine, and I felt my alarm growing. What had happened to my wicked boys? And why was I here with these two instead?

Then I remembered what else was missing.

Fuck.

Oh *fuck*!

"Looking for this?" he asked, a sinister smile playing on his lips.

Before I could demand answers, the King of Clubs reached down to his hip and drew out the Vorpal Sword. The gleaming blade seemed to hum with power as he lifted it up for me to see.

"Give that back!" I snapped, my heart racing.

But deep down, I knew I was in no position to make demands. What could I do against these two powerful men? And why did it feel like everything I'd been fighting for had just slipped through my fingers?

The King of Clubs merely grinned, his eyes gleaming with mischief as he sheathed the sword out of my sight.

"I'll give it back," he said with a sly smile, "if you play your cards right."

I narrowed my eyes at him, not wanting him to see how much he pissed me off and failing miserably.

"Fine. What do I have to do to get my sword back and get out of here?"

A cunning smile spread across the king's mouth. He held out his hand of cards to me, keeping the black and gold pattern facing me so I couldn't tell one from the other.

"Pick a card, then put it back. If I guess which one it is, then you stay until I say otherwise. If I *don't* guess the correct card, then you can take your precious sword and walk right out of here. Deal?"

"Sure," I nodded, glancing at the cards. There were a lot of them. At least twenty. I liked those odds.

"Deal?" he repeated, his tone more serious this time.

"Yeah, deal," I said, rolling my eyes at him. He ignored it and gave me a smug smile. That didn't surprise me at all, given that he was wearing a pinky ring.

"Pick a card."

I hemmed and hawed for a few seconds, then teased one out of his grasp.

"Look at it without showing me. Then put it back."

When I looked at my card, I snorted.

It was the King of Clubs.

Of course it was.

I slipped it between two of the cards and watched him shuffle them in his skilled fingers. He made them dance between his long digits like a magician. I'd never really cared for card tricks, but I had to admit, he was entertaining.

"Ready for me to guess which one is your card?"

"Bring it on," I dared, crossing my arms over my chest.

He lifted the very first card on top of the deck and showed it to me.

"This is your card."

My eyes widened and my jaw fell.

It was the King of Clubs.

"How did you . . . I don't understand how you . . ."

A low, wicked laugh rumbled through his chest as he fanned out all of the cards and let me see them for myself.

What.

The.

Actual.

FUCK?

They were *all* the King of Clubs!

"That's not fair!" I screamed at him. "You asshole! I never had a chance of leaving, did I? That's not fair at all!"

"I don't play fair, Alice," said the King of Clubs as he returned to the sofa and resumed his game with Callister.

"I play to *win*."

Pssst . . .
I need your opinion. Got a sec?

Leaving reviews is one of the most kickass ways to support authors. You're also helping other readers decide if our books are right for them. If you have a minute, I'd LOVE a review from you!

Review Ace of Spades on Amazon and/or Goodreads

Thanks so much!

Jekka

JEKKA'S WILDE ONES

Desperate for more?

Join Jekka's Wilde Ones!

Get immediate access to Jekka's private Facebook group, character art, the spiciest new Fantasy & PNR books, and be notified of new releases before anyone else.

Become a Wilde One at jekkawilde.com/newsletter

ABOUT THE AUTHOR

Jekka lives with her husband in the northern US, where it's cold most of the year. For someone who works from home, she has way too many shoes and not enough dogs.
She loves curling up with a warm blanket, a hot matcha latte, and an even hotter book boyfriend. Or *boyfriends*.

Because why choose when you can have it all?

Printed in Great Britain
by Amazon